# THE ADVOCATE TYE MONIQUE

Tye Monique

First Printing
978-1-943284-43-6 (pbk)
978-1-943284-46-7 (ebk)

A2Z Books, LLC Lithonia, GA 30058 www.A2ZBooksPublishing.net. Manufactured in the United States of America A2Z Books Publishing has allowed this work to remain exactly as the author intended, verbatim.

Cover design Devonia Lee

# DEDICATION

For Trent.
For Blaire.

-Love Always,
Mommy

# TABLE OF CONTENTS

# CHAPTER 1

# THE OVERVIEW

"Good Morning Students! I want to welcome all of you back to Lenwood High School for another successful school year. For anyone who may not be familiar with me, I am Principal Chutney. I have been the current Principal here at Lenwood for about three years now, and I have worked here for the past ten years. I am very familiar with many if not all of you. Along my journey in the education field, I have met great friends who also happen to become my colleagues. Some of you may know by now that Mrs. Stanson has retired-"

"Thank goodness," Jessica mumbled.

"Taking over her English classes will be my friend, my colleague I should say, Mr. Derrick McCall. Please welcome him and treat him with much respect."

"Jessica, do you see those big, brown eyes?!"

"Kristen, that is inappropriate! He is your teacher."

"You are absolutely right, but I absolutely can look."

Jessica shook her head in disbelief. Kristen had been her best friend for the past three years. She was a lot of fun and very outspoken. The two of them most definitely leveled one another out. Jessica did not open up to just anyone, and she kept a lot of her feelings to herself. Some of her peers considered her to be shy.

She was the co-captain of the varsity cheerleading team, so you would automatically assume that she was outgoing, but she really wasn't. Jessica was focused on her school work and making her way to college. English was her favorite subject, and she had planned on paying close attention in this class.

"Thanks to Mr. Chutney for such a warm welcome. Once again, I am Mr. McCall and I will be your eleventh grade English teacher. I have been teaching for eleven years, always at the High School level, and it has been an interesting experience. Every year is a different journey, which is great. I am really excited about being here at Lenwood. I have heard nothing but positive things, and that makes me look forward to a great school year ahead of us. I just quickly want to share a little about myself. I came from another High School here in Texas, not too far from here. I am truly a southern guy! I don't have any children, but I come from a really big family. Uh, I have high hopes for this school year, and if all of you help me, I know that we can definitely make good things happen."

Jessica was staring out of the window being easily distracted by the minimal activity that was occurring outdoors. She was thinking about the half-time routine that she needed to choreograph for the Homecoming game in a couple of weeks.

"Jessica DeLaney?"

There was a moment of silence.

"Is Miss DeLaney present?"

"She is right here! Jessica, snap out of it!"

"Oh, sorry. I'm here."

Jessica was somewhat embarrassed that she was not as attentive as she normally would be.

"Thank you for being here." Mr. McCall smiled.

Jessica opened her notebook and began rummaging through her syllabus. Her first day of junior year was already starting off rough, but she was determined to excel this year. Jessica's schedule was very hectic, and she had a lot of prioritizing to do. Robin, Jessica's mother, had a lot of faith in her daughter. She knew that she wanted to accomplish a lot after her High School years and she was going to stick by Jessica every step of the way.

Jessica's parents were newly divorced. She and her mother remained in their family home, and her father moved about 15 minutes away in a townhome community. It had been about two years but felt much less since they finalized their divorce. Jessica was still dealing with all of her frustrations and all of the new changes in her life. In the beginning, she would spend her weekends with her father up until he met his girlfriend last year. Martin, Jessica's father, had been planning on getting married – again! All he was waiting for was his daughter's blessing.

"So tell me about this school year, Jess."

"What do you want to know?"

"I don't know. Like are you prepared? Are you confident?"

"Mom, it was only the first day." Jessica laughed.

"Well excuse me for trying to make a conversation with my teenage daughter." Robin laughed.

"Is dinner ready yet?"

"Yep. We're just waiting on your father to get here."

"You mean dad's coming to dinner?"

"Uh huh."

"Why?"

"Truthfully, he invited himself. He said that he wanted to talk to us about something."

"He better not spoil my appetite."

"Be nice."

Robin and Martin were married for 15 years. They said those vowels at the sweet age of 21. While most people were anticipating being able to purchase alcohol legally, they were becoming a union and expecting the birth of their first child. They were very much in love and extremely happy throughout their entire relationship. Jessica would always want a strong marriage as her parents once had, but she never wanted the divorce.

"That must be your dad."

They made their way to the kitchen table and sat down to eat.

"Hey there! My favorite girl!"

"Hey, Daddy!"

"Are you too busy to spend time with me on the weekends now?"

"I've just been busy focusing on school and cheer. Plus, I am trying to find a job."

"A job? You knew she wanted a job?"

"Yes, Martin. We have discussed the job idea, and I think it is just what she needs."

"Why? Jessica, you are already busy enough."

"Daddy, I need to start making and saving my own money. I don't want to depend on you or Mom all of the time. I can handle this; I got it."

"I can't argue with you there. I support your decision, baby girl."

"Thank you. That really means a lot to me."

"So can we bless this food now?" Martin insisted.

Robin said the blessing as they all held hands. The aroma of the hot meal placed in front of them was tempting! There were hot, sweet rolls, baked chicken with homemade gravy, fresh collards, corn on the cob, and sweet potatoes. Robin had made all of Jessica's favorites.

"Y'all still eat good I see," Martin mumbled as he continued to stuff his face with chicken.

"Well, Martin before you fix another plate, can you explain why you asked if you could come have dinner with us?"

"Oh yeah. Well, you both do know that I have been dating Lisa for a while now."

"And???"

"AND… I am going to propose to her, but I want the two of you to back me up on this."

"Let me explain to you the reason why I cannot."

"Go ahead, Robin."

"Seriously Martin. I don't know her, and I don't see why I should get to know her. Jessica is 16 now and she is old enough to handle the relationship between you and her."

"I get it. There's still something else."

"I knew it," Jessica laughed.

"First thing's first, divorce does not mean that we are no longer a family. Robin, you and I have been around one another for 20 years, and I don't want that to change just because I am planning on getting married again."

"Don't you feel like we are still good friends, Martin? We get along, I still let you eat here, and I don't even poison your food. I say that we are doing great!" They all laughed.

"Well, Mama is coming to visit, and I want to tell her my plan to propose. However, I need the two of you to be there when I do decide to tell her."

"No thank you."

"Dad, you must be joking."

"Come on, Robin! You were my mother's only daughter-in-law, well in her mind, you still are. I just need you to help me get her to make that transition into you being replaced, well not how it sounds, but you know."

"Martin, I love your mother, but why am I being involved in this?"

"Please! Plus, she insisted that she stay here with you and Jess while she's visiting."

"Great. I love when Grandma visits. It distracts me from the two of you because this divorce has been nothing but weird."

"Martin, can you come into the living room for a quick second?"

"Yeah."

Martin knew that he was about to have an ear full! Robin had no problem expressing herself when she felt a certain way. Although they were now divorced, Martin and Robin made it extremely difficult for people to understand their relationship with one another.

"I'm sure this will be good."

"Martin Allen DeLaney, Jr. in the 20 years that I have known you I have never felt more used than I have for the last 20 minutes or so."

"Robin, don't you think you're overreacting a little bit?"

"You want me to be there to distract your mother so that she doesn't flip on you when you tell her that you want to propose to Lisa! Whom she has never even met!"

"What's the big deal?"

"You sound so juvenile right now."

"I just want to do things right. I want my marriage to work out because my first one sure as hell didn't."

"We both know that I am not the blame."

"Look, I am going to head home. My mother will be here on Friday. I thought maybe after we see Jess cheer, we could all go have dinner and talk."

"You sure love doing a lot of talking lately."

"Tell Jessica I will call her tomorrow. Good night, Robin."

"Good night, Mr. DeLaney."

Robin was so frustrated! She hated to feel as if she was being led on, especially by a man that she spent nearly the last 20 years loving. She knew that Martin did not want to get married again, but she wanted to still support him. It was exactly like what he had said at the dinner table, in the most awkward way, they were still a family.

"So are you ready for this half-time routine? Your first game as a choreographer and as co-captain!"

"My question to you is, do you know the routine?" Jessica grinned.

"A girl freezes up one game, and no one lets it rest."

They laughed. Kristen and Jessica had become sisters in the past few years. Being an only child was rough sometimes for Jessica. She felt as if she didn't have anyone to talk to unless she wrote it down. She was grateful for her best friend and their friendship that was evolving into a sisterhood. Kristen moved to Texas and they instantly became a walking diary for one another. Unfortunately, English was the only class that they had together this year, so they had planned on making that class time their personal gossip zone.

"Ok, the bell has sounded so I would like to go ahead and start discussing your first quarter project. It is an essay," Mr. McCall smiled.

"Principal Chutney may have schooled me just a little bit regarding this group and how you feel about writing essays. Trust me; I dislike grading them more than you dislike writing them. So we will get through it together."

"Jess, look at the way his lips flow when he starts talking."

Kristen was infatuated with Mr. McCall just as any teenage girl would be.

"Kristen, focus on what the man is saying instead of how he looks when he's saying it. We both know that you of all people need to be listening." Jessica joked.

"So let's start with a discussion on a topic for your essays. Uh, Miss DeLaney, could you think of a very challenging time in your life and how you faced the situation?"

Jessica became uncomfortable. She did not know any of these students, besides Kristen, well enough for her to open up about her personal life. She did not appreciate what Mr. McCall was doing to her.

"I…I didn't have my hand raised."

"Yes, I understand that, but I was hoping you could start the conversation and we could go around and piggy back off of one another."

Jessica wanted to take Mr. McCall's notepad and smack him across his face, but she was thinking about the future. When she goes to college, her Professor could call on her sporadically. So in a way, she should thank McCall for the preparation.

"The floor is yours, Miss DeLaney."

"My brother," Jessica paused. "My newborn brother passed away four years ago. He was four days old at the time. It was hard for me to deal with because I was grieving and I still had to console my parents. The entire situation was difficult for everyone and my parents argued a lot afterwards. A year later, they got a divorce, and I still believe that is the reason that they are no longer together. As far as dealing with the situation, I'm still dealing with it."

Jessica could not believe that she had just expressed herself the way that she did, but it was therapeutic.

"Well Miss DeLaney, thank you for sharing your situation. It truly was unfortunate what happen to your family. I am sincerely sorry."

Mr. McCall felt a sense of guilt for calling Jessica out on the spot, but he appreciated the honesty and the bravery. Ironically, the class ended. Jessica immediately grabbed her books and headed for the door.

"Miss DeLaney, can I have a minute with you, please?"

"Kristen, I'll meet you in the cafeteria in a few minutes."

Kristen walked alone to lunch hoping that Jessica would spill the beans about the entire conversation that she was about to have with Mr. McCall.

"I want to personally thank you. I did not mean to put you on the spot or anything like that."

"It had to be done eventually I guess," Jessica shrugged.

"That was an extremely touching story. Thank you for putting your heart out there the way that you did."

"No problem."

The silence became too intense for Jessica. She wanted to break out in a sweat! Those chocolate brown eyes were making her melt.

"Snap out of it, Jessica! This man is your teacher." She thought.

"Thanks, Mr. McCall, but I really should be going."

Jessica ran out of the classroom as quickly as possible. She maneuvered through the hallways with her head down. Once she arrived at the cafeteria, surely enough, Kristen was there anxiously waiting.

"Well, it took you long enough!"

"Don't ask."

"Umm excuse me, but you cannot have a private conversation with a sexy, new teacher and not expect me to ask questions. I am your best friend! It is my duty to find out what the deal is."

"There is no deal."

"Seriously, what happened?"

"He just apologized and told me that he appreciated what I shared with the class."

"That's it?"

"Yes!"

"No after school tutoring? No extra credit opportunities?"

"Quit it. That man is our English teacher and nothing else."

"Age is just a number."

Jessica could not believe that she was even having this conversation with Kristen. There had never been a thought in her mind about Mr. McCall in such a way. She could not take Kristen seriously. She needed to focus on her academics and being co-captain of the cheerleading team for the first year. She had been looking forward to that opportunity and did not want to let her teammates down.

When Jessica had gotten home, she was greeted by her Grandma, Sylvia.

"Jessica! My sweet baby!"

"Hey Grandma," Jessica smiled.

"I am so happy to be here with you and your mother."

"What about with Daddy?"

"Especially that father of yours."

"How did you get here?"

"Your mother picked me up from the airport. She had to go to her job for a little while. She said she would be back shortly."

"Got it. So are you ready for my performance tonight?"

"You better bet that I am. I cannot wait to see my favorite captain do her thing."

"Co-Captain."

"Same thing. We all know that Miss Jessica DeLaney has owned the varsity squad since her first day of try-outs."

Jessica laughed, "I love you Grandma."

"I love you too."

"Hey, hey everybody!" Martin announced himself from the kitchen.

"Mama!"

"Boy, don't you think you should be knocking? You do have your own place now."

"Well Mama, Robin and I have that type of understanding."

"What might that understanding be?"

"Oh, hey Robin."

"Child, wipe that sweat from your forehead." Sylvia laughed.

"Well, I'm going back to the school."

"We can't wait to see our favorite cheerleader hit the floor!"

"See you there, Grandma."

The minute that Jessica left, Sylvia cracked down on Martin and Robin.

"So, what is this game that the two of you are playing?"

"Game? Mama, what are you talking about?"

"Well, you surely don't act like any divorced couple that I know."

"Ms. Sylvia, we don't hate each other. Yes, Martin gets on my last nerve sometimes, but he is still one of my good friends."

"Plus Mama, I have to eat. Where else would I go for dinner?" Martin laughed.

"Well, why can't this girlfriend of yours make your meals? She doesn't sound too domestic to me."

"She's getting there," Martin insisted.

"Ok. I'm going to go grab my things so that we can head over to the school."

Robin wanted to change the conversation. She did not know Lisa personally, but she knew that she was not the right one for Martin. It was not to say that she wanted Martin back, but she wanted to make sure that the woman that he chose would be the one that he would spend the rest of his life with. As for Sylvia, she never believed that Martin and Robin ever dealt with the loss of their son in the proper way. In fact, both of their families believe that to be the cause of their divorce.

Meanwhile, when they had arrived at the school, the entire gymnasium was in a frenzy! It was the varsity boys' championship game, and even the local news station had shown up. Jessica was excited about her performance and nervous all at the same time. Also, she could not wait to see Brandon do what he loved doing, and that was playing basketball. She knew that Brandon Maverick would lead their team to victory. He was a well-known junior who was outstanding when it came to basketball. He and Jessica met in Junior High School and they instantly connected. Although they really liked one another, the friendship had been stagnant for a while now.

"I don't want to make you nervous, but good luck! Don't drop anybody or let anybody drop you." Brandon teased Jessica.

"Thank you for the thoughtful advice," she laughed. "I'll be sure to return the favor at half-time." Jessica smiled.

Jessica could see herself dating Brandon, but she didn't believe that it would turn into anything serious. They both had promising futures, and she was not sure if she wanted to compromise that at this point in her life. Still, Jessica wanted to enjoy time with her friend and to continue to see if their relationship had the potential to grow into something.

"Hello, Miss DeLaney."

"Oh, hey Mr. McCall."

"Nice crowd out here."

"It is! Everyone really came out to show our boys some support."

"What about the cheer squad? Everyone isn't here just to see the game."

Jessica gave him a frightening look that made McCall sense that she was feeling uncomfortable.

"Well, I better be going. The game is starting."

Jessica was getting ready to perform, but her mind was in a million and one places all at once. She was nervous to do their performance in front of her family, Brandon, and now Mr. McCall had made her feel much more awkward. Well, it was show time and that meant that the co-captain had to leave it all on the floor. The routine turned out to be great and everyone gave the squad a standing ovation! Jessica was beyond relieved, but this was one of her last routines until she became captain. That was the moment that she was preparing herself for.

After Lenwood High School earned another championship title, Jessica headed to dinner with the rest of the family. Her father was depending on Jessica and her mother to convince Sylvia to accept his engagement. Jessica didn't really have an opinion on her parents' love lives. She wanted nothing more than to have her family back together, but she was learning to accept what was already done.

"Jessica that was an amazing half-time routine! Had Grandma feeling like I was a teenager again." Sylvia joked.

"Well Grandma, they say that you are as young as you feel."

"I don't think that applies to Grandma," Martin mumbled.

"I beg your pardon!"

"Never mind him. Ms. Sylvia, you are stunning."

"Thank you, Robin. I knew that you were always my favorite."

Robin looked at Martin stuffing his face. She knew that he had been avoiding the reason why they were at dinner, to begin with.

"Martin, don't you have something to mention to your mother?"

"Don't tell me! Robin, are you pregnant?"

"Oh no! No, Miss Sylvia, Martin and I are no longer involved."

"Well son, what is it that you have going on?"

'Mama, I am planning on asking Lisa to marry me."

"Who?"

"Lisa, the woman I have been dating for going on 18 months."

'That child?"

"Mama, she's 31."

"Still not as mature as Robin. I mean, you said yourself that she doesn't even cook! So you are now saying to me that you plan on going over to your ex-wife's home every night for dinner?"

"Oh no!" Robin interrupted. "No offense." She smiled.

"I know that it may seem sudden, but she makes me happy. She is there for me and I know that she loves me. I'm asking you to support me as your son."

"Jessica, how do you feel about your father planning on getting married again?"

"Honestly, I don't know. I care about my dad and his happiness, but I don't need any new family members."

Jessica did not do well with change, and Robin knew that her daughter was beginning to feel uncomfortable. She wanted to rescue her daughter from hurt and pain. She knew that Jessica did not want to see her father married again, especially to Lisa.

"And Robin?"

"Well, I don't think that my opinion matters."

"Of course it does! You have been in Martin's life for 20 years and you were his wife."

"I just want Martin to do whatever it is that makes him happy, seriously."

"Martin, I respect that you care so much about me to ask my opinion. Of course, I'm not going to be anything less than honest with you.

I really don't see Lisa as marriage material."

"Well, maybe you can get to know each other better because Lisa is here. I asked her to join us."

"She's what?!" Jessica exclaimed.

"I wanted her to spend time with the most important women in my life."

"Dad, did you really have to do this tonight?"

Jessica was under a lot of stress. She was worried about landing the captain position on the cheer squad, dealing with Mr. McCall and his awkward ways, and she was stressing over Brandon. She had a lot on her plate and she did not feel like dealing with her father's relationship issues on top of all that. Jessica could tell that her mother wasn't happy about being at the dinner table right at this moment, and she wasn't sure if her grandmother was pleased either.

"Maybe I should go and let you guys finish up your meeting." Robin insisted.

"No. Robin, please stay. I really want Lisa to meet you."

Robin gave Martin a death stare. He was damn near begging his ex-wife to meet his potential, future wife. However, she was not prepared for any of this. Although they had been divorced for a couple of years now, Robin still felt a certain way about what was about to take place. She did not want to meet a younger female who was more than likely going to be her daughter's step-mother. Martin went over by the bar to escort a woman back to the table.

"Lisa, this is my family. You met my mother briefly."

"Yes, Miss Sylvia! How are you?"

"I'm well, thank you."

Martin could tell that his mother was not in the mood to converse. He was silently praying that she remained pleasant and polite throughout the remainder of the encounter.

"Lisa, this is the most important person in my life, this is my daughter Jessica."

"Oh my goodness! It is so great to finally meet you. Your father talks about you all of the time, and you are so beautiful."

"Thank you."

"And this is Jessica's mother, Robin."

"Hello, Miss Robin! I see where Jessica gets her beauty from."

Robin was still stuck on the fact that Lisa put a "miss" in front of her name. She did not say one word. Robin smiled and took sips of her Long Island.

"Well I don't know about you all, but I am ready to head home. Robin, shouldn't we be heading back to the house?"

"Oh, sure. Well, it was nice meeting you, Lisa. Mr. DeLaney, thanks for dinner."

Sylvia led Robin and Jessica out of the door. Martin was very heartbroken that he was not supported by the ones that he loved. This was not making his decision about proposing any easier. He wanted happiness again. He wanted to fill that void from 4 years ago when he and Robin lost their child. Martin clearly remembered holding their son in the hospital, preparing to take him home, but only for the doctor to tell them that he would not make it due to breathing complications. It was a drastic time that he doesn't believe will ever get easier to cope with.

Later that night, Martin went over to the house hoping to speak with Robin. He knew that she would probably be sleeping, but he also knew that she would give him some of her time. Robin was still Martin's closest friend, and she was still there for him whenever he needed her to be, but Robin wanted nothing to do with this engagement situation. She was tired of having to repeat herself, but it seemed as if that was what Martin wanted.

"Do you have the slightest idea what time it is?" Robin growled.

"Sorry, but I really need to talk to you."

"Martin DeLaney, we talk more now than we did when we were married."

"No jokes right now. Robin, why did the dinner make my decision more difficult to make instead of making it easier?"

"What are you talking about?"

"When my mother asked to leave and then all of you just left."

"I was the driver! Martin, what more do you want from me? You asked me to help you to convince your mother to support this engagement; I did that. Then you invite your future fiancé to dinner and expect me to be respectful, I was. I still give you so much of me to this day, and you could care less."

"You have always stuck by me and supported me. You and my mother. Why should that stop because we are now divorced?"

"You cannot have your cake and eat it too. You asked my opinion; I gave it. You can look right at Lisa and tell that she is not genuine. There is something about her that seems so fabricated, and you just ignore all of that. Then again, who am I to assume? I don't know her, and better yet, I am not the one that has to be married to her. I could be wrong."

"Yes you are."

"You asked and I answered."

"Why do you have to be so critical?"

"It's my opinion! Martin look, your life has nothing to do with me. In fact, I have tried to remove myself from it multiple times. You are the one who constantly wants me to be involved."

Martin knew that everything Robin was saying may have had some truth. He could not make up his mind about what he really wanted to do at this point in his life. It was time for him to figure it out and to no longer place the responsibility on Robin to do so.

# CHAPTER 2

# THIS AIN'T FOR PLEASURE

"Jessica, please tell me that you're going to the Winter Formal."

"I'm not."

"You can't be serious! The cheerleading captain must be there."

"I'm not even the captain yet."

"Co-Captain, captain... same thing! You gotta be there."

"Kristen, you know that I am not into parties."

"Well, you should be."

"Morning, ladies."

"Oh, hey!"

"Good morning, Brandon." Jessica smiled.

"You ladies ready for the Winter Formal?"

"Well I am, but maybe you can try and convince your friend Jessica here to attend because she obviously isn't listening to me."

"Really? Jess, you're not going?"

"I hadn't planned on going. Dances just aren't my thing I guess." Jessica shrugged.

"Well, that's unfortunate because I was looking forward to asking you to be my date."

Jessica could not speak one word out of her mouth. She was mesmerized by Brandon's smile and bright, brown eyes. She really wanted to change her mind on the spot, but she didn't want to seem too desperate.

"Why are you playing hard to get? You know that Brandon likes you and you won't even give him the time of day."

"I'm not even sure if he likes me."

"How straight forward does he have to be? The boy clearly just said that he wanted to ask you out."

"I guess you're right."

It was now time for English class, and Jessica was not looking forward to it. Things had been a bit uncomfortable ever since Mr. McCall approached her at the basketball game. She did not want to make a big deal, but she was pretty sure that he was trying to push up on her. Still, she didn't want to jump to any conclusions. Jessica just decided to keep her distance as much as she possibly could.

"Good afternoon, students. While we get prepared for today's lesson, I want to discuss the essays. I dedicated the majority of my weekend to grading 100 essays. I actually just got around to showering this morning," McCall laughed.

When he realized that the class was not receiving his joke that well, he decided to quickly change the subject.

"Tough crowd. Moving on, some of your essays were beyond me, and you deserve the public recognition for your outstanding work. The English Department will be hosting an essay contest with opportunities to have your essays advance to different levels, and I have attached a contest entry form to the essays that I would like to represent this class. If you are interested, just fill out the form and place it on my desk at the end of the class period."

Of course, there was a form attached to Jessica's essay. While she thought her essay was great quality, she did not like a lot of attention on her. She had some insecurities that she was still learning to deal with. Jessica considered herself to be shy. She filled out the form anyway and handed it to Mr. McCall at the end of the class period.

"Here you are, Mr. McCall."

"Thank you. I can't wait to see your essay progress. Really looking forward to it."

Mr. McCall was acting like a High School boy. Jessica had no idea why her English teacher was putting forth so much effort to be around her. She wasn't sure if she should take precaution or just play nice.

"Hey Jessica."

"Yeah?"

"You're the yearbook editor, right?"

"How'd you know?"

"Well, word got around that your group was looking for a new sponsor and I volunteered. I just wanted to introduce myself to the school's Editor."

McCall looked extremely suspicious! All of a sudden he wanted to be of "all things Jessica". She was wondering if anyone else had begun to notice all of the personal attention that he was showing her. What if it was starting to get around school? Jessica could not handle the pressure, but she believed that she could be overreacting.

"I better get to class."

"Sure. I'll see you during your yearbook meeting."

That was what Jessica was concerned about the most. The Yearbook Editor and the Sponsor had to have a lot of separate meetings, and she was not comfortable being around Mr. McCall alone. She could not imagine being left alone with this man for hours at a time, but she was not going to step down from being the Editor. She worked extremely hard to get to the position, and she was not backing down.

Things were still going strong for Martin and Lisa. Although he had not proposed yet, Martin was still planning on doing so. He had not seen Jessica or Robin since their dinner, and he had not called his mother since she had gotten back home from the visit. It was not out of spite, but they were all extremely busy with their personal affairs. Lisa admitted that she loved Martin, but she never really showed a lot of interest in his life or in his family. Martin wanted her to show more effort because he was very much involved and invested in making sure that his family remained a strong unit. Even the three-week period of not seeing or speaking to them was beginning to take a toll on him.

"Hey baby!" Lisa smiled as she greeted her man at the front door.

"Hey sweetheart."

"How was your day? I know you must be tired."

"A little bit."

Martin went to grab a cold beer from the refrigerator and looked around. There was nothing frying, nothing boiling, and nothing in the oven! Lisa did not even make her potential husband a sandwich. This had never really bothered Martin as much as it did tonight. Lisa permanently moved into Martin's home nine months ago, and she had been in between jobs since she moved in. Martin was starting to wonder what she did with so much extra time on her hands. He cleaned, he did the grocery shopping, and he paid the bills. It made him think about his life when he was married to Robin. Their marriage was not perfect, but Robin was a very good wife! She worked, maintained the household and contributed to the bills and expenses. Their marriage was a partnership and that was what Martin had hoped to have with Lisa in the upcoming years.

"That must be dinner."

Lisa made her way to answer the front door. Martin was through with eating out! It was either Chinese, pizza or something frozen from the freezer. Martin wanted a balanced, home-cooked meal.

"I got your favorite pizza, honey. Ham and pineapples!"

"Thank you, but we had a big pot luck at work today for lunch. I'll probably just take it to work tomorrow. You know what, I have to run back to the office. I left an important file that I have to look through tonight."

"Ok."

Martin headed straight for the door. He did not have to go to his office; he just wanted a break from his own home. He got to Robin and Jessica's house about 15 minutes later. (He knew what time they had dinner each night.)

"Hey Dad, long time no see."

"Hey baby! You too old for hugs now?"

Jessica hugged her father tight, the same way she did at five years old when she wanted him to chase away the monsters at bedtime. It was a sense of security when she was afraid, and it took all of her worries away.

"What brings you over here?"

"Well, I wanted to check and see if I had any mail, and I wanted to talk to your mother real quick."

"And…You're hungry." Jessica laughed.

Jessica shook her head as her father followed her into the kitchen. Although her parents' relationship was somewhat confusing, Jessica still enjoyed seeing them together whenever she could. It made her heart be at ease.

"Ma, look who I found at the front door."

"Why am I not surprised? Hey, DeLaney."

"Well, at least you're in a good mood. I came to see if I had any mail."

"It's over there on the counter. By the way, when is the change of address coming?"

"I just haven't had the time."

"In the past two years, you haven't had time?"

"Nope. Just like you haven't had time to go back to your Maiden name."

Martin gave Robin a sly grin. There was nothing else that she could say. They were so hot and cold with one another. Some would think that Martin and Robin were never divorced, but that was just the type of relationship that they had.

"The lasagna's ready."

Jessica popped up and ran to the oven.

"You made lasagna, Robin?"

Robin's lasagna was one of Martin's many favorites! His mouth was watering and everybody knew that he was not getting these kind of meals at home. There was the hot pan of lasagna, salad, garlic bread, Robin's famous sweet tea, and her cheesecake for dessert. Robin didn't have the time to cook each night, but when she did… she did!

"This is quite a meal for just two young ladies."

Robin looked at her ex-husband from the side of her eye.

"Sit down, DeLaney."

"Just say the word."

Martin blessed the food and did not give the lasagna a mere second to cool off before he piled up his plate.

"Daddy, if you're eating here, what is Lisa going to eat?"

"Oh don't worry, she'll just order a pizza."

"Translation, that's what she planned for their dinner and your father took off."

Martin nearly choked as Jessica and Robin laughed. He was so embarrassed and didn't want any of them to think that he had doubts about his new relationship. There may be a sense of uncertainty, but he was very much in love.

"Ma, don't forget to pick up your dress from the cleaners tomorrow."

"That's right! Thanks for the reminder."

"Got a new dress?"

"Yep."

"What's the occasion?"

"She has a date this weekend."

"Thank you, mouth! Well as Jessica said on my behalf, I do have a date."

"Must be a special guy if you're putting dresses in the cleaners. The last date we had you wore jeans."

"Jessica, let me talk to your father alone."

"Sure."

Jessica knew that her parents still had feelings for one another. Their relationship was weird and she never understood why they went through with the divorce as opposed to seeking counseling. She just wanted her family back together as a whole.

"Martin, stop with your games!"

"What are you talking about?"

"You come in here acting like you wanted your mail, but your hungry ass wanted a hot meal because your fiancé can't boil water."

"She's not my fiancé yet."

"Why did you feel the need to bring that to my attention?"

"Just making valid points."

"You're being funny and I don't see anything funny."

"Why do you need to date?"

"It's time! Why should I be by myself?"

"Are you honestly ready to date or are you doing this because I'm planning on getting married?"

"I don't know what world you're living in, but everything is not always about you! I deserve to go out and enjoy good company. I'm not sleeping with him and even if I were, that would be my business. Unless I invite you into my business, then you should have nothing to worry about."

Martin felt as if he was losing his best friend. He may not admit that he was jealous, but he was not ready for what could possibly happen after Robin started dating again. He made himself a plate to take for lunch tomorrow and headed towards the door.

"He better have you home by curfew."

Robin threw the dish towel at Martin's head as he left. She had never wanted them to lose their friendship no matter what the future would hold for both of them. They had history and plenty of memories. Robin had no reason to dislike her ex-husband. She wanted to keep the strong bond that they had always had. When Martin got home, Lisa was not there. Ironically, outside of her safety, he was not really concerned. Lisa really consumed a lot of her boyfriend's energy, and sometimes that was draining him. Martin enjoyed a lot of "manly" time doing things that were important to him. He enjoyed going to basketball games with the fellas and to the bar to have a few drinks. Those things were like a breath of fresh air at this point in his life. There were things that he enjoyed doing with Lisa as well. They enjoyed going to concerts and museums. Lisa was very expensive and that drove Martin crazy!

"Hey there, you're back." Lisa smiled as she entered the room.

"Yeah. I uh, got tied up when I went back to the office."

"I see. Well, there's plenty of pizza left."

"I'll save it for tomorrow, still full from the pot luck."

Whatever comment that Lisa would make, Martin was quick on his feet with a response. It was done in a very defensive way, and it was like Lisa was performing an investigation. This was not healthy on either of their behalf. Martin was ignoring this feeling, but he was starting to fall out of love with Lisa. Meanwhile, Robin was extremely excited about dating again, but also very nervous. For the past two years, she had been dedicated to building a new life as a single mother, but Martin was making it extremely difficult at times. Luckily, Jessica was older and understood more, but it still took a toll on their daughter.

"Hello, Robin DeLaney."

"Hey Robin, it's Curtis."

"Hi Curtis!" Robin smiled.

She sounded like a high school girl. Curtis worked downstairs in her building. He was the gentleman that Robin was really enjoying spending time with. It was nice to be out with a man after such a long hiatus.

"Have you had lunch already? I was wondering if you would join me."

Robin glanced down at the plate of food sitting on her desk and wiped her mouth.

"Oh no. I haven't gotten around to lunch yet. I would love to join you."

An hour later Robin met with Curtis at a local restaurant a few blocks down from their building. Curtis was very attractive! He was not the type that Robin normally pursued, but she was learning not to be so selective and leave plenty of room for change. In the past month, he had kept a smile on her face and had made small gestures that really imprinted on her heart.

"So how's your day going?"

"Surprisingly, it is going extremely well. My office is peaceful today which is fairly odd." Robin chuckled.

"Good to hear."

"How's your Friday going? Any big weekend plans?"

"Well, my children are coming to town for a few days. I figured I would spend as much time with them as possible."

"How old are they?"

"Curtis Jr. is 18 and Mallory is 16."

"Teenagers! I was one. I have one."

"Glad to see that someone's on the dark side with me." Curtis smiled.

"You are not alone. My daughter Jessica is 17 years old. She's the cheerleading co-captain, yearbook editor, and she wants a job."

"Busy girl. That should make you proud."

"It really does, but sometimes she can be a piece of work."

"I'm going to guess that she takes after her mother on that one."

"How so? Are you implying that I am a piece of work?"

"In a sense. I mean it took five attempts before you agreed to have lunch with me."

"Actually it was seven, but I applaud your tenacity." Robin smiled.

"You're such a beautiful, mature woman – inside and out. I respect that about you."

"Thank you. That really means a lot to me."

No one had complimented Robin in a very long time. It felt good! For a while, she had struggled with learning how to accept a simple compliment because it made her feel like every man was always trying to push up on her.

"So tell me more about Robin DeLaney."

"What would you like to know?"

"Your likes, your dislikes, your favorite foods, the simple things."

"Well, I'm a mother first. Jessica will always be my first priority. I am divorced, but my ex-husband and I still get along very well. We have known each other maybe 20 years, and we have come a long way with the co-parenting."

"If you don't mind me asking, how did you know that you were ready to date again?"

"Honestly, I don't know. I still am unsure sometimes if I'm actually ready, but I knew I wanted to get back out there gradually. I still believe it will be a while before I enter an actual relationship again."

Curtis began wondering if he should consider that as a red flag. He was not ready to jump into anything serious, but he was hoping that he would be the only one that Robin was dating. Little did he know, Robin was not going out with anyone but him from time-to-time. (She didn't even consider them to be dating.) She was just enjoying life and was moving at her own pace.

"Mom, can you help zip me up?"

"Of course. Oh, Jess! You look stunning."

"Thanks, but relax. It's just a dance."

"You're right. I can only imagine how I'll be when it's time for prom. My baby, my only baby, is really growing up."

Robin hugged her daughter tight and she did not want to let go. Jessica was her life! She knew that once she would go off to college that everything would be so different.

"I'll get the door. It must be Brandon."

"Baby girl!"

"Oh, hey Daddy. Thanks for coming to see me off. Unless you're here for other reasons." Jessica smiled.

Jessica really enjoyed stirring things up between her parents. She believed that somewhere deep inside of them that there was a part of them that still wanted to be married, but they were two very stubborn people.

"You know I couldn't miss my daughter leave for her dance. This is the pre-game for prom, graduation and you going off to college. By the way, this Brandon boy needs to hurry up so I can go over my rules."

"Rules?"

"Yes, rules! Dating my daughter comes with rules and requirements."

"Requirements? Dad, please don't embarrass me!"

"Martin, leave her alone! Now, stand over there so that I can grab a picture."

Brandon arrived moments later. He was very well groomed and had a mesmerizing scent. Jessica was in awe! She was head over hills for this boy, but had hoped that no one could tell. Martin was very impressed by Brandon's demeanor. He could tell that this young man had his head on straight. Every time that Jessica's parents had an encounter with Brandon, it was always pleasant. However, this time would be different because it was actually a date. Once Jessica and Brandon had left for the dance, Martin went to the kitchen. Robin stood in the middle of the living room looking confused. She gathered her thoughts and walked into the kitchen only to find Martin cutting a thick slice of pie.

"What's up?" Martin mumbled as he stuffed his face.

"Martin, we need to establish some rules since you love to establish rules for everybody else."

Martin looked concerned. He knew how firm his ex-wife could be.

"What do you mean by rules?"

"I mean you coming over here unannounced and you just going right into the refrigerator. You no longer reside here! I would appreciate the respect and courtesy of contacting Jessica or me before you walk in."

"Are you saying this because you want to have men come over?"

"Really immature, Martin! First of all, I am not in any serious relationship. If I were, that would be none of your business. You drew up the divorce papers, so you live with the outcome."

Robin did not want to sound angry, but she had held a lot inside over the past couple of years. She was a devoted and very loving wife. She loved Martin with every part of her. When she wanted to fight for her family, Martin called it quits. Now, he was trying to get back what he threw away. Martin wanted to talk to Robin, but he decided to let her cool off for a while. He had a lot to deal with and he wanted to do that on his own terms. When he had got home, Lisa was not there, and he honestly did not care at the moment.

He walked towards the refrigerator, grabbed a beer, and turned on the basketball game. Martin thought that alone time would give him plenty of time to reflect. It was coming up on the anniversary of the day that they had lost their son. This was a constant reminder of how easily Martin had given up. He remembered being there for the sonograms when they found out the gender. He also remembered how days after his only son, Jeremiah DeLaney, was born he sadly passed away.

Martin began to cry. The memories were replaying crystal clear. He remembered how Robin stayed in the nursery for weeks and did not say a word. The entire house was silent and everyone was saddened by the unfortunate outcome. Jessica watched how the death of her baby brother ripped her family apart. She saw her father come home at odd hours of the night, and she watched how her mother fell into a slight case of depression. Instead of seeking counseling or trying to communicate with one another, they just kept all of their emotions bottled up inside. Martin did not want it to be this way any longer.

Jessica and Brandon were really enjoying the dance. It was giving them plenty of time to get to know one another on a completely different level. Kristen was keeping her eyes on her best friend and her date, but ironically so was Mr. McCall. At the last minute, Mr. McCall volunteered to chaperone the dance. He was supposed to be supervising the entire student body, but his eyes were stuck on Jessica DeLaney. Jessica was too busy enjoying herself that she hardly noticed this man's eyes following her throughout the entire venue.

"Jessica, I didn't get the opportunity to let you know at your house, but you look absolutely beautiful tonight. I'm glad you decided to come with me."

"Thank you. To be honest, I'm happy that I accepted your invitation. I don't usually attend school dances."

"How come?"

"I really don't know. I just never felt the need to."

"Well, I hope that tonight leads to many other dates in the future."

"I would love that."

Brandon led Jessica to the dance floor as her favorite song played. This was like a fairytale. She became mesmerized by his masculinity and cologne. Brandon grabbed Jessica closer. She smelled of lavender. They wanted the song to last for an eternity, but savored the final 45 seconds. McCall watched from around the corner as Brandon placed his hands on Jessica's waist. He broke out into a sweat as he gulped about 3 cups of punch. Why would a teacher care so much? It was almost becoming frightening, but no one had noticed anything unusual. Jessica had felt uncomfortable at times, but she was not focusing on anyone else in the room. She was looking forward to spending the remainder of her night with Brandon.

"Jessica."

"Oh, hey Mr. McCall."

"You look really nice tonight."

"Thank you."

"Uh, do you need me to wait for your ride with you? I didn't see your car outside."

"No thank you. I'm here with Brandon."

"Good guy, really good guy."

"Hey, Mr. McCall."

"Mr. Maverick, you looking real dapper there."

"Thank you sir. Jessica, you ready to head out?"

"Sure."

"Well, don't let me hold you. You kids enjoy the rest of your night and be safe."

Brandon and Jessica headed to a nearby restaurant. They were really excited to get to know each other better. Two of the most popular kids in school were finally getting a chance to "just chill." Neither of them was a fan of attention, so it was nice to be secluded.

"I can't believe that it has taken us this long to even sit and talk. You have really made this night special for me. I'm honored to be your date." Jessica smiled.

"I'm glad you said yes because I don't think that I would have had this much fun with anyone else."

Brandon grabbed Jessica's hands and gazed into her eyes. All she could do was smile and close her eyes. Brandon then leaned in for a thirty-second kiss – leaving Mr. McCall admiring her from the restaurant's parking lot.

# CHAPTER 3

# MIXED SIGNALS

"Miss DeLaney."

"Yes, Principal Chutney?"

"There is a deadline coming up for the first draft of the winter section in the yearbook if I am not mistaken."

"That's correct."

"Could you schedule a time to meet with Mr. McCall this week so that we can get that taken care of?"

"Ok. Are you going to be attending? I can show you what the staff has accomplished so far this year."

"Unfortunately, I cannot, but just come by my office once you have everything together."

"Yes sir."

"Enjoy the rest of your day."

"Thank you, sir."

Jessica looked as if she had just seen a ghost! She did not want to be in a room alone with Mr. McCall, not even for a few moments. Physically, he had not done any harm to her, but it was just the way he made her feel so uncomfortable.

"Got any plans after school?" Brandon asked.

"Principal Chutney called a yearbook meeting."

"You want me to wait around for you? We can do something afterwards if you want."

As much as Jessica did not want to turn down Brandon's offer, she had to. She did not want Mr. McCall to sense that she felt uncomfortable. Ironically, she felt like that might caused him to make more and more attempts to push up on her.

"Umm, how about we have an ice cream date another day after school?"

"Sounds like a plan," Brandon smiled.

Jessica was extremely happy with the way that things were between her and Brandon. He made her smile more than anything else right now. She knew that she wanted their relationship to grow. Brandon was extremely happy as well. Although he was the most popular guy at school, he hardly ever had a girlfriend until now. He was excited to begin something new and to see where the two of them would go from here.

"Miss DeLaney."

"Oh. Hey, Mr. McCall."

"Did Principal Chutney speak to you about the deadline?"

"He did. You know, I could just e-mail everything to you and we could communicate that way. I know you're probably busy with all your other work and stuff."

"I think we should meet and get it out of the way. I have a few hours to spare."

Jessica wanted to curse! Nothing she said would get her out of this meeting. She had made up her mind that she would sit through the meeting and then tell Principal Chutney that she did not feel comfortable being a part of these meetings any longer.

"Kristen, I have to talk to you about something."

"What's going on? I feel like we haven't spoken that much in a while."

"Do you think that Mr. McCall flirts with me?"

"Say what?" Kristen laughed.

"Kris, I'm serious! I mean you know how he was at the basketball game and the way he was talking to me at the winter dance. Now, all of a sudden he's the Yearbook Sponsor."

Kristen had an awkward look on her face. She did not want Jessica to worry, but the way things were sounding she was starting to be concerned for her best friend.

"Jess, just relax. I am sure Mr. McCall is just being nice because he's a new teacher here."

Kristen was not even convincing herself at this moment. Jessica decided to put on her brave face and try not to overreact about something that had not happened.

"Maybe you're right. I'm just going to do my job as an editor. I have worked way too hard to let someone scare me away."

The remainder of the day went by so quickly. At the sound of the dismissal bell, Jessica and Brandon walked over to their lockers. She was doing anything in her power to delay her yearbook meeting. She closed her locker, hugged Brandon, and walked two doors down to Mr. McCall's classroom. She knocked softly, seeking permission to enter.

"I apologize, I never realized it was locked. Come in."

"Thanks."

"So, since I am new to this yearbook program, Principal Chutney informed me that you are the best person to go to."

"Ok. Well, what he asked me to do was submit all of the first winter season drafts."

"May I take a look?"

"Sure, here you go."

"Wow! You lead a really impressive team of future journalists. I am impressed."

"They work extremely hard and they are all very dedicated."

"Don't be so modest. You have to take some credit for being the Editor. I am sure you spent a lot of time critiquing these spreads."

"I did."

Jessica started to become more relaxed. She began to think that maybe she was jumping to conclusions about Mr. McCall and his actions towards her. She thought that his intentions were pure and that he was strictly about the business. This made it easier for her to get the job done as Principal Chutney requested.

"Well, I better be heading home."

"Oh, absolutely. I will let Chutney know that we accomplished everything during this meeting. Very productive."

"Sure thing."

Jessica grabbed her materials and headed for the parking lot. She survived! The sun was shining, her sunroof was open, and she was all smiles the entire ride home. She was so focused on playing it safe that she did not even notice Mr. McCall's Durango traveling about two cars behind her. He watched her pump her gas, he sat under the scorching sun as she made a stop at Rite Aid to pick up her personals, and finally found her home as she parked her car in her driveway.

"Hello?"

"Where are you?"

"What do you mean?"

"Derrick, you called me over here and you're not even home yet!"

McCall's eyes got so big! He had forgotten that someone special was coming over. She had planned to make dinner with all of his favorites. Derrick's mouth began watering just thinking about the meal.

"Baby, I almost forgot! I had a meeting after school, but I am on my way now."

"Hurry! I cannot wait to see you."

Derrick did nearly 85 mph all the way to his condo. This person had a key to his place for emergency purposes. They had been separated for only a short while, but she still lived nearby. Actually, she had just moved out of Derrick's condo about nine months prior. Being roommates and sexual partners without any distinct title was getting to be extremely difficult for both of them.

"Glad to see you still have that key."

"Flowers?"

"My apologies."

"For?"

"For not remembering that a very special friend of mine was coming over to cook for me."

"Seafood gumbo."

Derrick's eyes lit up! Gumbo of any sort was his favorite. He got a bottle of the best champagne off of the rack and poured two glasses.

"A toast."

"A toast?"

"Yes. To friendship, everlasting friendship."

"I will drink to that."

Derrick had a way with making any woman he was around feel special. Most women would consider him to be suave and debonair, but some see right through him and see how much of a slick, bastard he could be.

"So how is it going at your new school?"

"It's cool. This High School is a little different, but it's nothing that I can't handle. Have you found a new job yet?"

"Unfortunately, no. I have met a guy with hands in a major corporate company."

"A boyfriend?"

"Potentially. I plan to work my magic long enough to get my hands deep into his business; then I won't have to lift a finger for a while."

She and Derrick laughed constantly for a few moments. There was no humor in what she had said, but they were not taking anything seriously at the moment. Dinner was complete, champagne was flowing, and the rest was history.

Martin was finally ready to apologize to Robin for not respecting her space since he had moved out into his own home. He also wanted to ask her a really huge favor. Normally, Robin would do anything for Martin without hesitation, but since the dynamics of their relationship had changed he knew that it might not be easy.

"Hey, DeLaney."

"Hey, Robby."

"I hate being called that and you know it."

"That's what your colleagues call you. Curtis, right?"

"What does Curtis have to do with the reason that you're here, again?"

"I know that he's the man that has you buying new dresses and dying your hair. What are you on some "Waiting to Exhale", "How Stella Got Her Groove Back" shit?"

"First of all, I could never be Stella! Curtis is older than me."

Robin started laughing, but Martin was not appreciating the humor.

"What's the real reason why you're here?"

"I wanted to have a talk with you if you had the time."

Robin really was not in the mood to hear what Martin had to say. She felt that if he had been willing to talk this much during their marriage, then the divorce would have never been finalized.

"Can we do this over some food? I am hungry."

"Martin, this is my day off. I am not cooking anything upon anyone's request."

"No, no. I wanted to take you to breakfast. We need to go somewhere where you can't yell or curse me out."

"I only do that when you deserve it, and you're lucky because I have spared you plenty!"

"Come on, I'll drive."

Although it seemed a bit awkward for so many reasons, it wasn't unusual. After the divorce, Martin and Robin spent time with one another quite often. They wanted their daughter to have a sense of normalcy as opposed to a chaotic life. They did not want their personal issues to affect her. The two arrived at a Diner about 35 minutes north of their neighborhoods. It was two minutes from their Alma Mater. Martin and Robin had many dates there as struggling College students. They had some of the best conversations as well. Robin told Martin that she was pregnant with Jessica during their junior year in this very place.

"If these walls could talk."

"Right."

"So what did you drive almost 45 minutes to eat for?"

"Can we order real quick? I'm starving!"

"What? Lisa didn't have time to make breakfast on her way to the unemployment office?"

"You just had to."

"What did I do?" Robin laughed.

"You know what, let's disregard all of that."

They sat at the same booth that they had been sitting in for 20 years. Robin liked the view from the window. It allowed her to escape reality. She had set so many goals for herself sitting in that spot, and she could not believe just how long it had been.

"You know, the very first day we ate here, you told me that I would be stuck to you forever."

"I was determined, wasn't I?"

"You thought you were." Robin laughed.

"You had so much that you wanted to accomplish that I really felt like you were too good for me. You didn't need me."

"Why would you ever think that?"

"Do you remember Martin DeLaney from 20 years ago?"

"I do."

"Exactly! I was immature, indecisive, and was just all over the place. Then, we happened."

"Is that what it was? We just happened."

"No, do not start that."

"Start what?"

"You always turn my words around. You try to make me look like the bad guy."

"Well, that's never my intention. You make it seem like it's a bad thing that we were married, let alone had children together."

"How can that be when that was the best part of my life? You were everything I ever wanted. It's just unfortunate that we didn't work out."

Robin and Martin never really discussed the death of their son in such capacity. It was an emotional and sensitive subject that they normally would shy away from.

"Well, we were too eager to quit."

"I don't think I'll ever be completely ready to talk about that situation."

"Why not?"

"Robin, you and I know how much we were looking forward to expanding our family, especially knowing it was a boy."

"Maybe we should have kept it to ourselves a while longer than we did. Maybe we jumped the gun."

"We can sit here and discuss what-ifs until we turn blue, and as much as we want to deny it, this was meant to take place."

"So are you ready to go and start your new life with Lisa now? Start planning for children?"

"Children?"

"That's typically what a newly married couple does, especially when the woman has yet to become a mother."

"Well, we haven't gotten that far yet. I still have the ring."

"You what?"

"It's at my place in the safe."

"I'm confused. Months ago you rolled up in the kitchen nearly begging me to get myself and everyone else on board with this engagement. I sat through dinners and smiled in a woman's face who I really could care less to get to know. Now you're going to tell me that the damn ring is still in the box!"

Robin was clearly frustrated, but she couldn't figure out what was really causing the frustrations. If she could be honest, she was happy in a way. With the proposal not happening, it still gave her some time to sort out some unresolved feelings.

"I'm going to do it, but when I do it, I don't want the first bit of uncertainty. I want to be completely sure just like – just like when I proposed to you."

"Well, I can tell you what you can stop doing. You can stop comparing our relationship and our marriage to what you're attempting to build with Lisa. That's not fair to any woman. It's not fair to anyone involved."

"That's true, but I guess I am trying to piggy-back off of what I know that worked. I mean, I am too close to 40 and if this relationship doesn't work, then I'm not thinking marriage ever again."

Martin and Robin sat for another hour. The dishes were cleared, and there was nothing placed on the table but their thoughts and emotions. On the way home, they sang their favorite songs from when they were in college. Martin kept all of their favorites in his collection. Robin shifted her body and stared out of the window as she sang multiple songs. Martin tapped the steering wheel to the beat a few times. You could hear the pain and the cry the entire car ride – coming from the speakers.

Jessica and Brandon had been very busy with their personal activities that they were barely spending any time together. It didn't change their feelings, if anything they grew stronger. They were finally able to spend a Friday night with TV, pizza, cookies and anything else that their athletic bodies wanted to partake in. Jessica's parents allowed Brandon to come over, but this was something new for all of them. For the record, they were only now 17 years old. Fortunately, Jessica could be trusted and they assumed that Brandon could as well. In a sense, he could be trusted up until those teenage hormones started to run crazy.

"Can you believe that the two of us finally have a night to just be together?" Brandon smiled.

"I know. I couldn't wait for practice to be over so that we could do this."

Jessica was a very attractive young lady. To Brandon, she was beautiful and her personality was the best part about her. She could make him laugh on his worst days and make every stressful situation seem so small. What Jessica loved about Brandon was how attentive he was to her dreams and aspirations. He wanted to see her prosper in all aspects of her life and he constantly reminded her of that without saying a word.

Being that they were only teenagers, the last thing that Jessica wanted to do was make permanent decisions based on temporary situations. She knew that in a little over a year they would most likely end up on two separate ends of the country. However, she was becoming tired of always "preparing for the future." Jessica wanted to continue to live in the moment, even if that meant sitting on her sofa in her sweat pants and loading up on pizza.

By now, Mr. McCall had made a name for himself at Lenwood High School. Most of the students looked forward to his class. He was very well-known in only a short amount of time. However, there was one colleague who felt that something was a bit unusual about Derrick McCall and her name was Angela Thompson. Mrs. Thompson was one of the guidance counselors at Lenwood. She had been in the school system for 22 years and had witnessed a lot!

The students were just like her own children while she was at work, and she wanted to make sure that she did everything she could to assure them a prosperous future. Angela knew better than to assume anything without discovering the facts. She was not accusing Mr. McCall of anything inappropriate, but what she was going to do was keep her eyes and ears open and her mouth closed.

"Hey, Mr. McCall."

"Hi. Ms. Thompson, right?"

"That's correct."

"Oh, excuse me, Mrs. Thompson." Mr. McCall corrected as he and Mrs. Thompson shook hands.

"I didn't want to get too deep into the school year without speaking with you and making sure that this has been a great adjustment for you."

"It has all been great. These are an amazing group of students."

"That they are. And I want to thank you for hopping on and sponsoring the yearbook committee this year."

"No problem. Thanks to Miss DeLaney, I'm learning a lot."

"Miss DeLaney? Oh, Jessica. She is really a bright student all around. She is extremely passionate about Journalism."

"You are absolutely right. The passion is there."

Mrs. Thompson wasn't too sure how to receive Mr. McCall's comments. She did not want to take anything out of context, but she was taking mental notes.

"Well, I better get going. If you ever need anything, please do not hesitate to call on me. My office is right across the hall, literally."

Mrs. Thompson sent plenty of warning signs to Mr. McCall to let him know that she would be keeping her eyes and ears open. She was still stuck on the comment that he made about passion. No teacher had ever been that intrigued by an individual student before in her opinion. She wanted to speak to Jessica about the encounters she and Mr. McCall had been having, but once again, she did not want to make assumptions. Mr. McCall was not intimidated at all.

She may have been overreacting and she knew that she could not prove any irregular behavior just yet. This meant it was time for some private investigation to be done. When Mrs. Thompson left, it was time for the yearbook meeting. Brandon had weight training, so he was going to stick around until Jessica was finished.

"Good Afternoon, staff. I am not going to take up too much productive time by talking, but I want to congratulate you all for beating another major deadline. I know this is the busiest time of the school year, so there is so much to cover. At this time, Jessica will say something if she would like and then she'll give you all your next assignments."

"I really don't have too much to say except thank you. I should have just about all of the assignments situated in a few minutes. Once we get those out, we can end the meeting and we can start working immediately."

Jessica had strong leadership skills and she was extremely fair. She thought about owning her own magazine one day, but just like any other teenager, a new career idea popped into her mind each day. Robin and Martin constantly reminded Jessica that she could go do anything out in the world and that she was not limited to Houston, Texas.

"Really good meeting. You know you're beginning to impress me more and more each meeting, Miss DeLaney."

"Thanks."

"You know, you are just the type of person that I need to assist with my business ventures."

"You have your own business?"

"It's an upcoming project. Once I get the logistics worked out, I would love for you to check everything out and let me know what you think."

"You want me, a 17-year old to tell you what I think?"

"Why do you sound so surprised?"

"I don't know. I guess I'm just trying to figure out how I would be so beneficial to your business venture."

"Rule number one in making it in the real world: Never doubt yourself! Don't let your age or anything discourage you from achieving anything. Besides, I just wish that you could see in yourself what I see in you.

CHAPTER 4

# TAKEN FOR GRANTED

Lisa was still going on multiple job interviews each day. Truthfully, she was in no hurry to be back in the working world. She would much rather have Martin take care of her and spend her time doing things of her own personal leisure.

"Hey."

"Oh, hey. What's going on?"

"I'm in need of a favor."

"What's in it for me?"

She laughed. She knew that she could always run to him when she needed his assistance.

"What do you mean?" She smiled.

"You're asking me for a favor, what do I get in return?"

"Can we discuss that AFTER you help me?"

"Go ahead."

"I want to become a substitute teacher at your school, and I was wondering if you would help me do so."

"You?"

"Yes, me! Why does that seem to surprise you?"

"In all of the years that I have known you, I have never thought you took a liking to working with kids."

"In the beginning, I didn't. Then, I would see how passionate you were about teaching, and I have truly become inspired. Those students need more educators like you in their classrooms. You really build a connection with them and help them to see and understand the world from such a different point of view. That is why I really believe that I could be a great Substitute Teacher, based on what you have shown me."

Derrick appreciated the heartwarming compliments that he was receiving, but he knew that Lisa had her own itinerary. He thought that this was a new way for her to keep track of his personal life. Technically, Derrick was the single one and Lisa was not. Although the two of them were not currently sleeping together, she still felt as if she was the only one who was supposed to be in a relationship.

"Did you do the application?"

"Yes sir! Mr. McCall, I am on it. There is a long-term position available at your school, and I know you'll talk to Chutney for Me." she smiled.

"What do I get out of doing all of this work?" Derrick laughed.

"That can be our little secret."

Derrick kissed her and she let herself out. She had Derrick right where she wanted him. She knew that being a substitute would buy her some time until she could figure out how she would become part owner of her new man's business.

The next day was a normal day for Jessica at Lenwood High School. She was really getting stressed out about the annual cheerleading competition. This would be the first year that they were doing a routine choreographed by her. Jessica was nervous!

"I cannot wait to go to the competition just so that we can lounge around the hotel and see cute valet boys."

"Kristen, what about going to actually WIN the competition?"

"Oh yeah. Well, that's obviously the most important part, but lighten up. You cannot stress anymore about this routine."

"This routine could be the reason I do not become captain."

"Don't worry about any of that. You have it in you to be the best at what you do. Just always remember that."

Kristen may joke around a lot, but she was the epitome of a best friend. Sometimes Jessica felt guilty that Kristen was always so busy helping her with her issues and she didn't always return the favor. Kristen had moved to Houston nearly three years ago when her

Grandmother had gotten sick. Her Grandmother raised her nearly all of her life. When she took ill, Kristen moved with her mother and sadly enough, her Grandmother passed away last year.

"Do you ever wish that you could move back to Georgia, Kris?"

"More now than ever. I guess I'm just afraid."

"Of what?"

"Being there without my Grandmother. That woman made me who I am. The bitter, the sweet. The good, the bad. I'm not ready to go back and deal with that pain."

Jessica had learned quite a bit about Kristen's family over the years. Her mother had gotten married when Kristen was three years old to a man in the Military. That's when Kristen's Grandmother told her daughter that she felt like that lifestyle was too busy and insisted on keeping Kristen in Georgia with her. Jessica had met Kristen's mother on numerous occasions. She was a really nice lady, but she and Kristen were not as close as Jessica was with Robin. (Not to compare the two.) She could tell that Kristen loved her mother, but she knew that nothing compared to the relationship that she once shared with her Grandmother.

Jessica was extremely close to her family, but she had been seriously thinking about moving away for college and staying away. Of course, she would come to visit her parents for the holidays. If she was lucky, her father would not be with Lisa by then and he would have moved back with Robin. That was her wish. In fact, if she and Brandon decided to further their relationship, he would most likely be drafted into the NBA. She could picture herself in the near future. She would be writing sports columns about the man that she loved. Her headline would read: "Born a Maverick."

"What are you daydreaming about?"

"What else? My future."

"It is just too early to stress over anything."

"I'm not stressing. I'm just wondering if Brandon plays a part in it."

"Do you want him to?"

"Don't ask silly questions."

"No, seriously. At this point in your life, do you see Brandon in the picture when you think about your future?"

"I do. I guess. It doesn't even matter because I don't even know how he feels. After graduation, we probably won't ever see each other again."

"What has gotten you so worked up that you're so concerned about your future?"

"I don't know. Time is just moving extremely fast and I want to be prepared."

"No, you want to be perfect, and we both know that we are too young for perfection."

Kristen dealt with her issues behind closed doors, and sometimes she regretted not opening up to her friends and close family. However, she did know that she did not want to spend the rest of her High School years stressing over things that she could not control.

"Hello, I'm here to see Mr. DeLaney."

"Do you have an appointment?"

"Are you serious?"

"Ma'am, Mr. DeLaney's schedule is extremely busy. The best I can do is try and get you an appointment for later this afternoon."

"You must not know who I am."

"I don't, but I do know that I am about to close the office for lunch. So you're going to have to try again later."

Denise had been Martin's secretary for years! She was family. Over the years, she had helped to create a lot of success for Martin's business. She and Robin had been best friends since before college. They were sisters. She had been there from the birth of Jessica, the deaths, and the divorce. Denise still felt like Martin and Robin belonged together. She felt like they should have tried counseling as opposed to divorcing so quickly.

Lisa was still standing there in disbelief that the secretary would not call Martin and let him know that he had a visitor. She then noticed Robin walking in and a new set of emotions started to evolve.

"Hey Denise."

"Hey girl."

"Ready for lunch?"

"Just about. I just want to send this e-mail."

"Oh, hey Lisa. It's nice to see you again."

"Hello. Surprised to see you here. You and Martin having lunch? Did I come at a bad time?"

While heading to the restroom, Martin noticed both Robin and Lisa in the waiting area. He nearly broke into a sweat as he walked over to Denise's desk.

"Hey everybody."

"Hey DeLaney." Robin chuckled.

"Lisa, baby, what's up?"

"What's up? I needed to speak with you, but your lovely secretary informed me that you were booked."

"I can; I can chat for a second. Robin-"

"Don't worry. I'm just here to meet Denise for lunch."

"Got it. Well, you ladies enjoy."

"Want anything?"

"Nah, I'm going to skip lunch, but you ladies enjoy and take your time. I have everything covered here."

The ladies left and Lisa followed Martin to his office.

"Did you really just do that?"

"What?"

"You pretty much gave your secretary the rest of the day off."

"I did not. Besides, Denise works extremely hard around here."

"After how she treated me in the waiting area she deserves to be fired."

"Huh? Don't you think you're overreacting?" Martin laughed.

"I don't think I am. You want someone to represent your business that disrespected the woman you're in love with?"

There was a brief silence.

"Judging by the lack of response, I can understand how you really feel."

"It's not that! Lisa, Denise is family. She was there with Robin and me when we started this business."

"Here we go!"

"What's up with you today?"

"Your ex-wife constantly being a part of your life is what's up."

"You can't be serious. You know my history with my marriage and all that I went through. Don't try to erase that part of my life."

Lisa walked over by the window and stood there. She knew that there was no way she could fully gain control of this business with Robin still having partnership.

"You know, you're saying a lot to me right now that I can't fully grasp. I'll just see you later."

Martin had no energy to argue at the moment. He'd felt so drained by Lisa lately. He noticed a change in her attitude and the way that she had started to treat him. He had been ignoring the signs because of him dealing with his personal issues. This made his decision to propose more difficult. How could he marry someone who he wasn't sure genuinely loved him?

Robin and Denise ate lunch at the Mexican Restaurant a few blocks away. They did not want to spend their time talking about Lisa, but they both knew that the encounter would be brought up sooner than later.

"I still can't believe how Miss Lisa acted in the office earlier."

"Denise, are you sure you didn't give her a hard time because you knew who she was?"

"Shut up, Robin." They laughed.

"Seriously. You're just like Martin's mother. No one wants to accept that Martin and I are divorced. Even if it's been two years and we have both moved on."

"Well, maybe it's because the two of you aren't very convincing."

"I can't believe you just said that."

"I can. I mean come on Robin, can you completely deny that you and Martin haven't acted like the two of you were never divorced?"

"It may seem that way sometimes, but we are still raising a child together."

"I get it. Believe me, I am not judging either one of you, but as your friend, I just think you all should clear the air so that when you do move on, you can move on without any strings attached."

"What are you referring to?"

"Well, have you guys thought about counseling since the death of Jeremiah?"

Robin felt her heart sink in. She remembered every feeling and emotion that she felt during the life and death of her baby boy. Have you ever had to bury your child? Have you ever had to hold your son's cold body in your arms as he lies there lifeless? No breath in his body. All of those emotions and feelings struck her all at once. She was still grieving, no matter how much she wanted to deny it.

Denise wanted closure for her friend and the entire family. She wanted Robin to think about her late son and smile sometimes. She wanted her to remember the beautiful baby boy that God gave to her family, if only for a little while. She wanted her friend, her sister to truly understand that God makes no mistakes. It was dark in all of their lives at the moment, but she was banking on the promise that better days were to come.

When Denise got back to the office, she decided to have a talk with Martin. She knew that Robin was too stubborn to express her true feelings because it was Martin that actually filed for divorce. That was something that Robin would resent him for the rest of her life.

"Hey. Did y'all have a good lunch?"

"Yeah. It was nice to catch up, you know?"

"I'm sure Robin had a healthy serving of Martin."

"No!" Denise laughed.

"That woman doesn't cut me any slack."

"Well, Martin I want to first apologize for the way I acted towards Lisa earlier. It was not professional and it was childish."

"Hey D, don't sweat it."

"No, no. At the end of the day, I just want to see you and Robin happy. I guess I just never thought that the two of you would be searching for new happiness in someone else."

"That makes two of us."

"Then why did you file for divorce?"

"What was I supposed to do? Was I supposed to come home from work every day to a cold house? Was I not supposed to grieve so that my daughter could have one parent who wasn't depressed? I had to hold my shit together when the truth was that I was torn up inside and out! Why couldn't my boy make it?"

Martin slid down in his chair and nearly drowned in his own tears. He never really talked about the death of Jeremiah. Even after it was all over, Martin worked and kept himself busy. There was so much pain within every member of their family. Denise remembered how she got down on her knees each night and prayed for this family. She still continued to do so. She watched Martin and Robin press on each day, and while some days were more difficult than others, she knew that one day they would receive the peace they had hoped for.

"Martin, I had spoken to Robin earlier, and I know that you're divorced, but do you think that maybe the two of you could consider going to counseling? So you could finally move on in peace?"

Martin sat and thought about what Denise had said for over an hour. He knew that he was jacked up from the inside out, he knew that he was hurting and he knew he regretted filing the divorce papers. That decision was something that he was going to have to deal with for the rest of his life. He acted out of emotion, and although he may not admit that he regrets the divorce, he wished it hadn't happened the way it did.

Martin made a few phone calls and was able to set up a same-day appointment with one of the best Family Therapists in the Houston area. He sent Robin an e-mail to see if she was available on such late notice. Against her better judgement, Robin agreed to meet Martin at the therapy session. She had no idea what was about to go on, but she was preparing her heart and mind for what could occur.

"Hello, hello. I am Dr. Washington. It's very nice to meet both of you. Mr. and Mrs. DeLaney, correct?"

"It's Ms. DeLaney, we're divorced."

"Yes, I do see that in my notes. Got it. Well, Mr. DeLaney, you filled out the notes on the application so I'll go ahead and hear a few opening words from you."

"Well, one of our mutual friends thought that we should seek professional help because of some of the things we went through during the time of our divorce."

"If you don't mind me asking, what was so significant about that time?"

"We, we lost our son."

Martin felt a huge lump in his throat. He was headed in a direction that he was not able to turn around from.

"Was this your first child?"

"No. We have a 17-year-old daughter," Robin interrupted.

"Sounds like to me that you all have some years."

Robin felt a tear roll down her face. She just wanted closure!

"Martin, tell me about the death of your son."

"It was just dark. We prepared ourselves for the birth. We were very excited because we hadn't been new parents in 14 years at the time. Uh, we just really wanted a son and God blessed us with one. We sat in the hospital and within hours, I was holding this strong, baby boy in my arms. I passed him to my wife, my daughter held his hand, and within minutes the Doctor told us that we had some issues, "Martin cried.

" Days had gone by and by the time I worked up enough nerve to hold Jeremiah again, he was lifeless. He was dead!"

Robin remembered exactly what Martin was saying. It was a sad movie constantly replaying in her head. Every word, every detail that Martin described was all true. She reconnected with those emotions and just cried silent tears.

"Robin, what can you say about your pregnancy and during the time that you gave birth to your son?"

"One of the happiest moments of my life. Honestly, I was nervous because I knew that I was older than when I had given birth to my daughter. I was 35 and I knew that age also meant more risks. I went to my appointments and it wasn't until my final appointment when they told me that I had to deliver immediately. That was when I knew that it more than likely wouldn't be good. I just prayed and cried out to God to wrap His arms around my baby. To protect him. Then, when Jeremiah didn't make it, I knew that I didn't do something right."

"Are you saying that you blamed yourself?"

"I have for a long time."

"Martin, were you aware that Robin felt this way?"

"Not really."

"Well Robin, was there anything that Martin said or did that made you blame yourself for the death of Jeremiah?"

"Not particularly, but I do feel like his attitude towards me changed. I mean there were days when we would barely say a word to each other. There were a lot of dark nights and the next thing I know, he shows up with divorce papers."

"So Martin, you filed for the divorce?"

"I did."

"Then, why did you want to come to counseling?"

"I believe that at the time, I acted out of emotion. I guess what I wanted to happen was for the papers to be a wakeup call to Robin and let her know that she was not the only one hurting."

"You didn't feel like you could go to your wife and ask her if the two of you could seriously talk about what you were going through?"

"This was the first major issue in our marriage and I guess I didn't know how to handle the situation properly. I didn't think it through."

"And I'm not placing the blame on anyone here. Just so we are clear. Robin, when Martin handed you those papers, how did that make you feel?"

"I was numb. It was just another loss in my life. A year before Jeremiah's passing, I lost my parents in a very bad car accident. So when that pregnancy test was positive, I felt like I was getting some of my happiness back. Then, my baby boy dies, and within a month his father hands me divorce papers. This is the man that I devoted so much of myself to. I supported his dreams and did whatever I could to make them happen. How could someone who made a vow do that to me? I would have never run out on him! Not like that. Not at that time."

Martin felt like a piece of shit! Hearing that time replay in his mind gave him the chills. He caused this woman more heartbreak than she needed. He was not there for her like a husband of 15 years should have been. Now he was begging his ex-wife to seek counseling two years after he shoved a divorce down her throat.

"I do want to continue next week, but before I go, I want to know, have the two of you began new relationships?"

"I'm just casually dating, but nothing serious."

"I'm actually preparing to get engaged."

"Well Martin, how do you expect that potential marriage to manifest when the way that you ended your last marriage was so messed up? Think about that. I'll see you all next week."

Dr. Washington grabbed her files and left the room. Robin was still very emotional. In a way, she was angry. She just could not believe that the man that she devoted herself to left her during the most difficult times of her life. She didn't want to have hatred towards Martin; she had forgiven him for all of the pain he caused her. She just hoped there would be a day when she would wake up and not blame herself for everything that took place.

# CHAPTER 5

# MANIPULATION

Jessica was starting to feel comfortable around Mr. McCall in her English class and at the Yearbook Club meetings. Mr. McCall was finally starting to treat her just as he did his other students. In a way, Jessica was happy, but she was also a little upset about it. She was confused! Why should she care about the amount of attention that her teacher was giving to her? Education was the primary reason why she attended school each day and the fact that she still wanted more and more attention from this man was beginning to complicate things.

Jessica ignored how mesmerized she was by the way Mr. McCall stood in front of the class and had everyone so engaged. She didn't pay any attention to the way he smiled with his eyes and the way he used his hands to explain something whenever he was passionate about a specific topic. She didn't notice a thing! Who was she kidding? All of a sudden, Jessica had become head over hills for someone she stood no chance with.

"Snap out of it, Jessica! It's just a silly crush."

"Are you talking to yourself?" Kristen whispered.

"Huh? No."

"You were talking to yourself, Jess. Snap out of it." Kristen laughed.

Jessica wiped the smudge of drool from around her mouth. She could not believe how she was acting lately. She grabbed her project requirements and prepared to leave the classroom.

"Mr. McCall,"

"Yeah?"

"I was going through the project requirements and there were some questions that I had."

"Go ahead."

"Well, could we talk about it at a later time? That way you could show me some more examples of projects from previous years."

Derrick began to laugh silently to himself. He had Jessica exactly where he wanted her, but he was not going to reel her in just yet. She was a vulnerable teenaged girl who was starting to be manipulated by a coward. A 34-year old man became infatuated with a 17-year-old girl. He was just waiting to capture all of her innocence.

"Uh, Miss DeLaney, Kristen seems to have a good idea about the project. Why don't you go ahead and check with her and the two of you can let me know if you have any questions."

"Of course."

Jessica made her way down the hallway. She stood with her back to the locker and daydreamed. There was nothing in particular to think about, but she needed a distraction from what just happened a few moments ago. She had never been rejected by anyone for any reason at all! How could a teacher reject a student from receiving extra help on an assignment?

"Hey, J."

"Brandon, hey!" Jessica greeted him with a passionate kiss on the lips in front of everyone.

"Woah. What was that for?"

"I'm just really, really happy to see you." She smiled.

Brandon had noticed a change in Jessica lately. She had become more open, not that it was a bad thing, but he was just used to his girlfriend being more conservative. Brandon could get adjusted to Jessica's new personality, but it was still something unusual.

"Want to grab something to eat after school?"

"I'd like that. Or we can go to my house. My mother won't be home until late tonight." Jessica grinned.

"What kind of invitation was that?" Brandon laughed.

Jessica felt like she was being rejected by someone that she was in love with. Grant it, no one really took a teenage relationship seriously, but suddenly Jessica considered herself to be a woman. She was a new woman now and had a 34-year old man doing anything in his power to pursue her. Lately, Mr. McCall hadn't been showing that much attention to Jessica and it was starting to take a toll on her. How could this be? How could she care so much about a man who violated her with his eyes?

Jessica was confused and manipulated. She really thought that she would eventually start a serious relationship with her English Teacher. Now, where does Brandon come into the picture? Unknowingly, Jessica was beginning to treat Brandon unfairly. Slowly but surely, she was turning into someone who no one was able to recognize.

"Well, the invitation still stands. If you choose to accept, I'll see you at my place around 7."

Jessica kissed Brandon once again and strolled down the hallway. Brandon was completely sprung! As any teenage boy would, he wanted to go over to Jessica's house later that night, but he wasn't sure if the two of them were ready to take things to the next level. His hormones were racing, but he knew that this was not the right time to be intimate. Brandon knew that Jessica was still a virgin, and he wasn't sure if he should be the one to change that. There were a lot of emotions involved with being intimate at such a young age.

Later that day, Jessica went past Mr. McCall's room and did a double-take. Was that Lisa? Jessica wiped her eyes to see if what she was seeing was misleading, but sure enough, it was Lisa. She was smiling from ear-to-ear as she gazed into Derrick's eyes. This clearly was not a professional meeting. Jessica never took her eyes off of them as she gathered her notebook from her locker.

"You dropped something."

"Oh, Mrs. Thompson. I was just looking at how much that lady resembles my father's fiancé. It actually is her."

"I see. Your father's fiancé is in Mr. McCall's room?"

"Weird."

"Uh, Jess, take your notebook and head to class. We don't want you to be marked tardy."

"Yes ma'am."

Mrs. Thompson was taking mental notes. She was beginning to be very observant. Jessica couldn't believe how she was acting. If she was not careful, she would start some serious speculations. There was a lot at risk with this situation, and it was time that she took that into consideration.

"Derrick, did I tell you how happy I am that you got me this long-term substitute position?"

"I think we both realized that after what you showed me last night." Derrick laughed.

"I'm serious. But if you keep up the good work, I'll show you some more gratitude later on tonight." Lisa smiled.

Martin and Lisa hadn't been on the best terms lately. They were barely speaking to one another lately, let alone sleeping in the same bed. In fact, Lisa had been spending most of her time over at Derrick's house. (She says that it's more convenient for work.) Derrick was enjoying having Lisa around more. He had someone to cook for him, wash his clothes, and having sex on a regular was the icing on the cake.

"Well, I better get back to my classroom." Are you going home right after dismissal?"

"I have a yearbook meeting, but it won't be long."

"Well, I'll see you later tonight. Don't keep me waiting."

Jessica spent the rest of her day wondering why Lisa was at her school, let alone in Mr. McCall's room. She knew how Derrick could get when he sees a woman that he was interested in, and she wanted to make sure that her father was not being disrespected in any way. Was that all? Was that the only reason that Jessica wanted to know why Lisa was at her school? Maybe she considered Lisa to be a threat. Maybe she felt that now Derrick McCall would show Lisa all of the attention that he was trying to show her not too long ago. Whatever the truth was, Jessica was determined to find it out.

Robin was going on a date with an old college friend, Copeland Carter. He was in town on business and ran into Robin a few days prior. Martin and Copeland have never gotten along! (That's because he knew that Copeland was attracted to Robin). There wasn't anything that Copeland wouldn't do to get Robin's attention back in college.

Honestly, that is what turned Robin off. She didn't like a guy who was so focused on gaining her attention. She liked a guy who was more laid back and who let the chemistry happen on its own. She knew that is what attracted her to Martin the most. As much as she hated to admit it, she and Martin connected on so many levels. Nothing was forced! That's how she believed any attraction should work.

"So Mom, what is this guy Copeland like?"

"I really don't know." Robin shrugged.

"So you're going out with a stranger?"

"Girl, no. We just haven't seen each other much or talked much since we were in college. It's not like a date; it's like we're catching up."

Jessica admired her mother for so many reasons. She thought of Robin as her hero. This wasn't just because she was her mother, but this was because of the qualities that Robin displayed. She was a strong, loyal, grown woman! Robin was committed to all of the people in her life. She wanted to see everyone that she loved go after all of their heart's desires.

"What are your plans for the night?"

"I've been dealing with a lot at school lately, so I think it's best to just stay in and chill."

"Well, make good choices. You can always stop by your father's house if you get that bored. I know that they don't have much going on over there." Robin laughed.

Bingo! Jessica knew that this would be the perfect opportunity for her to get more information. She wanted to know why Lisa's been at her school so much the past few days. Plus, she wanted to figure out just how well Derrick and Lisa knew one another. She had some time before Brandon was expected to be at her house, so Jessica decided to pay her father and his "potential fiancé a visit.

"Hey, Daddy."

"Jess! This really is a surprise."

"I don't think I've been over here since you moved in. I like what you've done with the place though."

"Thanks. Lisa put her spin on it a little once she got settled in."

"I see."

Jessica hadn't been to her father's home since her parents divorced. Originally, her parents agreed that Jessica would spend a few nights a week with Martin, but things turned left once he began to date Lisa. Jessica made it very clear that she was not ready to be living around either one of her parents' new significant others.

"So what's up? What made you stop by?"

"Well, mom went out with an old college friend, so I figured that I would stop by and check up on you. Just to see what you've been up to."

"Does this old college friend have a name?"

"Copeland or something like that."

"Copeland Carter! How'd your mother hook up with him?"

"She said that they ran into one another a few days ago and he asked her out." Jessica shrugged.

Martin started to get angry. He remembered how many times Copeland would work overtime to get Robin's attention. He made it very clear that Martin never deserved a woman like Robin. Now that the two of them were divorced, Martin was sure that Copeland had his own agenda.

"So what is Lisa up to?"

"She's upstairs getting ready for her Girl's Night. You know that she's a substitute teacher at your school now."

"Really? I'm surprised that I haven't seen her around."

Jessica knew exactly what her father was talking about. She just wasn't aware that Lisa was actually at the school working. The question now was, how does she know Mr. McCall? (Not that it was any of Jessica's business.)

"So how did it go?"

"What?"

"The proposal."

"Oh that. We haven't gotten around to the proposal yet."

"I don't get it."

"Sweetheart, as you get older, you will learn to be more patient and more certain before you act on something."

Jessica sort of understood what her father was trying to say. It made her think of the plans that she made with Brandon for later that night. The timing was not right for them to make that move. She really cared about Brandon, but it was time to start thinking about risks versus the reward.

"Oh, hey Jess! I didn't know you were stopping by."

"Hey Lisa. I just popped in for a minute."

"Good to see you. I can't believe that we haven't run into each other yet. I'm working at your school now."

"Dad just told me."

"We'll have to get lunch one day."

"Sure."

"Well, I better get going. Jess, what do you think about this dress? Too much?"

"I like it."

"It's a bit much for a Girl's Night Out."

"Oh baby, relax. The girls and I haven't been out in a while so don't wait up."

Lisa leaned over and kissed Martin; then she paraded out the door.

"Dad, you have your hands FULL!" Jessica laughed.

Even Jessica knew that Lisa was not going out with her girlfriends dressed the way she was dressed. It was hurting Martin and his daughter was now starting to realize that. She knew that she had been busy and that she hadn't spent much quality time with her father lately, so she decided to cancel her date with Brandon. They both were honestly relieved.

"You're not going out tonight?"

"No. I had made plans, but I cancelled them. I'm just not in the mood to hang out."

"What about going to dinner with your old man?"

"Sure."

"I'll go get ready. I finally get some quality time with my baby girl."

Jessica enjoyed making her parents smile. She knew that they had been through a lot in their lives, and she just wanted to see them happy no matter what. Oddly, she knew that her parents still wanted to be together. They had a weird way of expressing their feelings, and Jessica was now just starting to come to terms with the divorce. Martin drove his daughter downtown to a really nice restaurant. The weather was great so they requested to sit by the water.

"Dad, this place is amazing! I'm so glad we came."

"Me too. Getting some quality time in with my only daughter is like pulling teeth these days."

Both Martin and Robin still say that they have two children. They do anything in their power to keep Jeremiah's name alive.

"Do you ever wonder what life would be like if Jeremiah were here right now?"

"We would probably be at Chuck E. Cheese or somewhere." Martin laughed.

Martin tried to bring light to a heavy situation because this was the first time that Jessica had even mentioned Jeremiah to him. He couldn't imagine breaking down in front of his child right at the table, but it could possibly happen.

"Baby girl, I think about how different our lives would be in the best way possible. I would have loved to have my boy here and watch him ride his bike, play his sports, talk about girls, and I can't do that."

Martin caught his tears before they fell down his face. He knew that Jessica was a lot older now, and more mature. As far as he was concerned, if he and his ex-wife owed anyone an explanation, it was to their daughter.

"You know sweetheart, your mother and I have been going to counseling sessions for the past month, and it has been helping with all of the things that we've had to deal with. The mistake we made was, we never considered your feelings with all of this, and for that, I apologize."

"I mean, I do wish things would have gone the other way. I saw how happy all of us were when we were waiting on Jeremiah to be born, and it's crazy how all of that happiness slipped away. It's like it died along with him."

Martin watched his daughter cry, and he knew that he had to allow her to heal in her way. It was amazing how someone that they had only known for such a short amount of time made such an incredible impact on all of their lives. While they sat there with a great amount of pain resting on their table, Martin recognized two familiar faces inside at the bar.

"Jess, I'll be right back."

"Ok."

"Can I get you a drink, sir?"

"Just a Coors, please."

"Martin?"

"Robin, oh what's up? And you have a very old friend out with you tonight I see."

"DeLaney, it's been a long time."

"Copeland Carter. I see you're still going after my belongings."

"Robin told me the two of you were divorced."

"We are." Robin interrupted.

"Look, Robin is a grown woman, and she can speak for herself. I'm going to grab my drink and get back to my beautiful date. The two of you enjoy your night."

Robin and Copeland watched as Martin walked back to the table.

"She looks a little young for him, doesn't she?"

"That's our daughter." Robin smiled.

It warmed Robin's heart to see Martin and Jessica sitting at the table together. It almost made her a little jealous that she wasn't included. They were still very much a family unit, and nothing could change that. Since it was getting late, Martin decided to drop Jessica off at home and have her pick her car up in the morning. As they were pulling up to the house, Robin pulled in beside them.

Martin knew that there was an unfinished conversation that he needed to have with Robin. Besides at the restaurant, they hadn't seen each other since their last counseling session. Even then, the two of them barely held a conversation. Jessica walked into the house before Robin had a chance to get out of her truck. Martin wasn't sure what type of mood Robin was in after he popped up at the bar, but it was time for him to check in on his ex-wife and see what she had planned for her relationship with Copeland Carter.

"You scared me!" Robin jumped as Martin knocked on her passenger side window.

"Can I talk to you for a minute?"

"Right now? In the car?"

"Won't be the first time." Martin smiled.

Robin unlocked the door and Martin jumped in.

"So how was your date?"

"It was nice. Crazy how my ex-husband and our daughter show up at the same location."

"It was a total coincidence. Seeing you actually caught me off guard, especially with Copeland Carter."

"It was just two friends out on a simple date."

"You don't have to explain yourself to me. Like you said, you're divorced."

"I constantly repeat myself because we're doing too much without any boundaries."

"We ain't sleeping together."

"Martin, you know that this is deeper than that."

"So is the fact that you're dating Copeland! You think he's not trying to get at me?"

"Why would he?"

"He goes after everything that belongs to me."

"Getting back to that, when did I become your belonging? I really didn't appreciate that."

"You know there was absolutely no disrespect from that. I'm sorry, I was wrong."

"It's cool, but we both know it better not come out your mouth again." Robin jokingly punched Martin in the arm.

"You know, being at dinner tonight with Jess made me realize just how much she's growing up. She asked me tonight how I felt about losing Jeremiah, and I almost lost it! It made me realize that she's really a young adult now and we've sort of neglected how she's been feeling these past couple of years."

"I have to protect my baby. She's the only one I have left."

"Pretty soon she'll be out on her own and then we won't have anything that ties us together. Breaks my heart."

Robin had to admit that Martin was making a couple of valid points in this conversation. Now that they were divorced, they only communicated when it would involve Jessica, as it should be. Truth be told, they both had issues with moving on into new relationships. Martin still had the engagement ring locked up in his safe. He and Lisa were definitely in an awkward position right now.

"Martin, you don't think that you and I could still be friends even as Jessica gets older?"

"You're going to treat me like a complete stranger!" He laughed.

"I can't believe you would say something like that."

"You have been shady towards me since the divorce."

"If you feel that way, I'm sorry, but who could be shadier than you? You served me divorce papers while I was dealing with the death of our newborn son! You have no idea how it feels when the person that you need the most turns their back on you."

"I'm sorry. I've done everything in my power to show you that I've tried to correct the mistakes that I made. But did you consider the fact that I was hurting too? He was my son too!"

"Neglecting your feelings was never my plan, Martin. Where were all of these conversations while we were still married?"

# CHAPTER 6

# UNWANTED ATTENTION

Kristen and Jessica hadn't spent much time together lately outside of cheerleading. This was unusual because they normally spent a lot of time over each other's houses or on the telephone all hours of the night. Kristen had always been there for Jessica whenever her friend needed her. Not that it was expected, but Jessica did not always give the same in return. Yes, they were young and it was only so much that they could go through as teenagers, but Kristen was going through a lot that Jessica had no idea about. All of their drama in their personal lives was starting to cause tension in their friendship.

"You and Brandon going out tonight?"

"We're supposed to, but I just haven't been in the mood to go out lately."

"Does someone else have your attention?"

"Why would you say something like that?"

Jessica started to get paranoid! She knew that Kristen sat next to her in English class and she knew that she didn't miss a beat. Kristen paid close attention to detail at all times. This all had Jessica thinking that maybe she even noticed that Mr. McCall was back preying, and this time Jessica was not holding back.

"I'm just saying, it is strange that you're passing up a lot of time with your boyfriend."

"I'm just really stressed! We have the yearbook conference in San Antonio next week to pick up our final draft, and then final exams won't be too far behind."

"How long will you be in San Antonio?"

"Couple of days."

"The entire staff goes?"

"Yeah, and McCall."

"McCall?"

"Mr. McCall, he's the sponsor."

"I get it. I just didn't know that the two of you were so informal."

"We aren't. It just came out in an unusual way."

Kristen knew that there was something different happening with Jessica and Derrick McCall. Things were no longer professional and it was starting to create major concerns. Kristen wasn't going to jump to conclusions just yet, although Jessica wasn't being a decent friend at the moment. She wanted to do anything in her power to protect Jessica from Mr. McCall.

"Good afternoon, ladies."

"Hi, Mrs. Thompson."

"Hello, Mrs. Thompson."

"You ladies have any major weekend plans?"

"No."

"Just getting everything done for the yearbook."

"Oh yes! That reminds me, I am your second chaperone for the conference."

"Great!" Jessica smiled.

Kristen was laughing on the inside because she knew that Jessica expected McCall to be the only adult on the entire trip. Truthfully, that was exactly what Jessica had on her mind at the moment.

"Well, you ladies enjoy your weekend, and I will see you on Monday."

"Kris, I'll call you later. I have to be somewhere before Brandon and I go out tonight."

Kristen was so confused. Why was her friend acting this way? She saw Jessica rush to her car and pull off, but she drove the opposite direction of her house. Kristen thought about following her friend to make sure that she was safe, but she decided to wait until she received a phone call from her friend later on.

(Knock! Knock!)

"Who is it?"

Jessica knocked again.

"What are you doing here?"

"We need to talk."

"You are really brave to show up at my house."

"You gave me the address to use. Did you not?"

"I gave it to you, but you should call me first."

"Look, I'm sorry, but you had already left when I came by your classroom. I need to talk to you."

"Jessica, you cannot pop up at any given time! I have a lot on the line with all of this."

"For the past six months, you have done nothing but try and get my attention, and now I'm here! I'm risking my reputation, my relationship with my parents, my relationship with a boy that I love, but I'm here!"

Jessica was literally in tears. How could she open up to someone that she hardly knew? Now that Jessica was giving herself to Derrick, he didn't want anything to do with her all of a sudden. He had gone up to his room for a quick second and came running down the stairs moments later.

"Where did you park? Jessica, where is your car?"

"Calm down. I parked at the shopping center around the corner."

Jessica was trying to figure out what was going on until she heard a car pull into the driveway.

"Look, go down in my basement and don't say a word! I'll come down in like 10 minutes to let you out the back way."

Jessica was disgusted! She had no one to blame but herself. She was not ready for an adult relationship.

"Derrick. Derrick, are you home?"

"I'm in the kitchen."

"There you are. I went by your classroom, but you had already left."

"I left early today. We're going to San Antonio on Monday, so I took some personal time."

"Am I invited?"

"This ain't for pleasure. You know I'm going for the Yearbook business."

"What am I supposed to do until you get back?"

"Work on ending that relationship with this Martin guy."

"That's nothing at this point."

Jessica was livid! She could not believe what she was hearing. She wanted to call her father and tell him everything that was going on right at that moment, but she would be in a chaotic mess if she did. Moments later, she heard footsteps come down the stairs.

"Jessica," Derrick whispered.

Jessica did not respond. She wanted to grab the closest object and hit Derrick in the head with it. When he turned around, Jessica was staring right in his face.

"Ahh!" Derrick screamed.

"How do you know Lisa?"

"Look, that's not important. You've got to get home."

"You've got a lot of nerve to shove me in your basement like some old piece of furniture!"

"Lower your voice! Look, we can talk about this when we get to San Antonio."

"Not with Mrs. Thompson there."

"We'll talk about it later."

Jessica rushed out of the door as soon as her cell-phone started to ring. She decided to call Brandon once she had gotten settled in at home, but to her surprise, he was there waiting on her front step.

"Hey."

"Finally! I've been calling you since school ended."

"Sorry. I was out job hunting. I was going to call you once I got back home, but here you are."

"I was worried about you. I haven't heard from you all afternoon."

Jessica loved how much Brandon cared about her. She couldn't figure out why she was dealing with Mr. McCall behind his back. Technically, she wasn't cheating because she didn't sleep with Derrick. Jessica wasn't having sex with anyone, and she knew that her relationship with Mr. McCall would never be more than a secret between the two of them.

"Brandon, let's go inside."

When Jessica walked past him to open the door, Brandon smelled a unique scent. He couldn't figure it out, but he knew that he had smelled that same scent before.

"You want something to drink?"

"Could I have a glass of water please?"

"Sure, I'll be right back."

Robin had sent Jessica a text saying that she and Denise were going to an event tonight. This gave Jessica some much needed alone time with Brandon. On the way back from the kitchen, Jessica had noticed that Derrick's cologne had rubbed off on her. She was hoping that Brandon hadn't noticed.

"Hey Brandon, I'm going to run upstairs. I'll be back in a few minutes. Make yourself at home."

Jessica used her mother's bathroom to shower so that Brandon couldn't hear what she was doing. Brandon was starting to wonder what had gotten into his girlfriend. He smelled the cologne and it was starting to stress him out. Jessica knew that she had to go downstairs and get Brandon's mind off of the familiar scent just in case he had noticed it. She ran over to her mother's closet and saw a brand new lingerie gown. If her mother knew that her 17-year-old daughter put on her brand new gown, Jessica would be dead! The question was: Who was Robin saving that special attire for?

"Sorry to keep you waiting."

"Jessica, hold on we need to-"

Jessica made her way over to the love seat and Brandon was completely distracted.

"You were saying?"

"It was certainly worth the wait," Brandon smiled.

Things began to get heated within seconds. Brandon had so much that he wanted to say, but for that moment, he was about to make love to his girlfriend for the very first time. There was a lot of uncertainty, but he was going with the flow. Jessica led Brandon up to her bedroom. She had no idea what she was about to do, but after being rejected by Mr. McCall earlier, she knew that someone deserved her love. Luckily, Brandon came prepared for the occasion, although he did not expect things to heat up right away. Jessica enjoyed every moment. Each minute was another magical moment and every tear was a memory. The next few days were quite difficult for Jessica because it was now time for her to go to San Antonio for the yearbook conference. Mrs. Thompson was watching her like a hawk! Any move that Jessica made, she was right there.

"Mrs. Thompson, I'm so glad that you came along to help chaperone. I really appreciate it."

Mrs. Thompson knew that Mr. McCall did not mean a word that he said. She knew that he had a separate itinerary of his own and she was ready to block any opportunity to put that into play, at all costs. Jessica spent the bus ride talking to Brandon and listening to her music. They had become a stronger couple these past few days. It was nearly strong enough to take Jessica's mind off of Derrick. Mr. McCall couldn't help but think about how he almost got caught up at his home just the other day. It was embarrassing to Derrick that he had taken such a strong liking to Jessica, a teenager.

It was evident that the two of them would never be on the same level in life. Jessica had a long journey ahead and Derrick was experienced. He had been married and gained a lot of knowledge about women through it all. As far as he was concerned, the heart wants what the heart wants. They had countless conference sessions as soon as they hit San Antonio. Then, they were finally able to take a break and have dinner.

Last week when Jessica had shown up at McCall's house, he gave her a cell-phone for them to communicate without anyone else knowing. They were investing a lot into this secret situation, and it was starting to get more complicated. They exchanged text messages during dinner for about 15 minutes. Apparently, Mr. McCall had reserved a separate hotel room for him and Jessica to meet up in later on that night. Mrs. Thompson did her room checks around 10:30 that night, then she headed back up to the fourth floor. Derrick instructed Jessica to meet in room 208 around midnight. He told her that he would head down soon after and would only knock once. Jessica did as she was told and she even bought a brand new lingerie set, similar to the one that she took out of her mother's closet.

"You are so bad," McCall smiled as he gazed at Jessica in her red gown.

"Only for you," Jessica giggled.

Derrick grabbed Jessica by the waist and tackled her to the bed playfully. Touchdown! This was the moment that Jessica had been waiting for. She wanted this man in the worst way. Her mind was on a rollercoaster ride as she laid there, and Derrick was in full control. Jessica knew that Derrick had plenty of experience because he was doing things to her that she didn't even know existed. There were a few soft moans, a few tears, and then reality snapped in.

"Here I go," McCall whispered.

Jessica felt totally different from when she slept with Brandon. She didn't say anything to Derrick, she just went back to her hotel room and took a shower. She put the gown in the garbage and scrubbed the make-up off of her face. Within minutes, she was back in her sweat pants and t-shirt with her hair tied up in a bun. She couldn't believe what had been going on for the past few months. It was time for her to fix her mistakes, but it could be too late now. Mrs. Thompson noticed how quiet Jessica was on the way back from San Antonio. She was deeply concerned, but she needed the proper support for her accusations. Mr. McCall was being his normal self, but he was worried that Jessica was about to blow their cover.

"Snap out of it!"

Jessica didn't respond to the text messages that McCall was sending. She didn't even make eye contact with Derrick for the next few days.

Lisa was still going through life on her agenda. She had something to do and that was to get Robin to sell her the other half of Martin's business. Robin was a pretty rational person, but she could handle her own. She did not know that Lisa would be stopping by her office, but she was always prepared to back herself up.

"Can I help you?"

"I'm here to see Robin DeLaney."

"Your name, please?"

"Lisa Johnson-McCall."

Robin's secretary went towards Robin's office to see if she was available. Robin had a confused look on her face, and she was certainly not about to come out of character at her place of business.

"Ms. McCall, you can go back. It's the first door on the right."

"Thank you."

"Hello Lisa."

"Hi. I'm sure you weren't expecting me."

"Not at all, but have a seat since you're here."

"Thank you."

"So what's up?"

"I don't want to hold you because I know how busy you are. Especially since you have your hands in two businesses."

"Excuse me?"

"Well, I know you're doing your thing here, and then you have your share in Martin's business. So I decided to come with a proposition."

Lisa handed Robin a hand-written check.

"Who the hell is Derrick McCall?"

"That's my brother. He's been nice enough to give me the money for the down payment to purchase your share of Martin's business."

"What? I don't know what you and your brother thought, but my share is not for sale. So you can write checks all day long, but you are wasting your time. Martin and I started that business together, and that is separate from our personal relationship."

"You'll do anything just to give yourself hope that you'll get Martin back, but that ship has sailed. My man is very well taken care of."

"See, I was doing just fine minding my business and not worried about you or Martin. Then, you have the nerve to come into my place of business acting like I'm supposed to jump for some money! Lisa let me explain something to you; there isn't anything you can tell me or show me about that man that I don't already know, and probably know it better than you. And if you were taking care of him instead of trying to buy me out, then maybe your man wouldn't be at my door damn near every night. Or maybe he would have given you that engagement ring that's been locked away for months!"

Robin ripped up the check and threw it away. Lisa was at a loss for words. She never wanted anyone to get her out of character. She wanted to go down to Martin's office and let him have it, but she was going to play it smart instead. Lisa removed herself from Robin's office without announcing her exit. Her plan was not working out as she had planned, and she also found out some new information about her boyfriend's whereabouts lately. However, Robin was sure to get to the bottom of the business scandal.

Back at Lenwood High School, Jessica had put herself back into a shell. She wasn't opening up to anyone, and it was starting to make Brandon wonder if she wasn't pleased with their romantic encounter a few days back. It was also starting to make Mr. McCall wonder if Jessica was about to let the cat out of the bag. Brandon sat at his desk in McCall's class with his mind elsewhere. This distracted Mr. McCall because he was wondering if Brandon knew about him sleeping with Jessica back in San Antonio. He had to cover his ass and wanted nothing to jeopardize his reputation.

"Brandon, can you stay back for a couple of minutes? I just want to talk to you real quick."

"Ok."

Brandon always felt a bad vibe from Mr. McCall. He just never felt like he had good intentions, and he suspected something when it came to Jessica. Brandon wasn't about to share any of his personal business with his teacher, but he was certainly going to be a listening ear. Brandon stood near McCall's desk once the rest of the students cleared out.

"So what's going on? You seemed distracted the entire class."

"Just a bad day, man."

"You know, you can always come talk with me. I know that I'm your teacher, but I can be a listening ear too."

Brandon smelled a familiar scent that distracted him.

"Is that your air freshener?"

"Oh, nah. Well, it's my cologne. I spray a splash of it in the room after each class to get rid of all those funky teenage odors," McCall laughed.

Brandon had a vein ready to pop out of his neck! That was the same smell that Jessica had on her the night that they had sex. Brandon was about to get to the bottom of the situation, but he wasn't sure how things would end up between him and Jessica.

"I gotta go."

Brandon left Mr. McCall's classroom in a hurry and drove over to Jessica's house. When he got there, he called and asked her to come outside to talk. Jessica was somewhat confused being that Brandon did not mention that he would be dropping by when they were at school.

"Hey."

Jessica got in the car and noticed this frustrating look on Brandon's face.

"What's wrong? Tell me what's going on."

"Jessica, the night that we ended up sleeping together, why were you in such a rush to go up and take a shower?"

"What type of question is that? I had been at school all day and I wanted to freshen up."

"When I came over, the plan was to just chill and relax. We even agreed that we weren't ready to take the next step."

"You didn't stop it from happening. Brandon, please tell me what's going on."

"What's going on is we both know that you went up to take a shower to get that damn cologne off of you! The same damn cologne that McCall wears! I knew I remembered that scent."

Jessica started to feel like her life was over! She had worked extremely hard to be responsible and to be credible. She wanted to put the situation with Mr. McCall behind her, but at this point, it may be too late.

"Brandon, what are you trying to say?"

"Cut the BS, Jessica. Just tell me the truth. Are you messing around with the teacher?"

"We had sex once, but not that night! You were my first, just like you wanted to be."

"That's not enough! You're out here sleeping around with a teacher! That's a lot of heat."

"It's over! I'm not associating with Mr. McCall anymore."

Jessica couldn't believe what was taking place, and neither could Brandon. She started to get emotional and just wanted to go back up to her room to be alone.

"We both obviously need some time to get ourselves together. You can call me later if you want to."

Brandon was emotional as well. On one hand, he was hurt, and on the other hand, he knew that this entire situation needed to be reported. It was time that legal action be taken. A lot would happen if Brandon opened his mouth to anyone else, so he decided to get another input on what he should do. Kristen met up with Brandon a couple of hours later that evening. She had no idea about what transpired, but she had been suspecting unusual activity between Jessica and Derrick McCall for quite some time now. When Brandon told her that he needed to meet up in a hurry, Kristen prepared for the worst.

"Hey, B."

"Thanks for meeting up with me."

"You look terrible! Is something going on?"

"Let me explain."

"Sure, go ahead."

"Two weeks ago, Jessica asked me to come over. Honestly, I didn't think any heavy stuff would go on because Jessica had told me a few days prior that she just wasn't ready."

"Right."

"We on the couch, we're cuddling, and I smell this masculine scent on her neck. It was a scent that I had smelled before, but it wasn't anything that I wear. So Jessica tried to play it off, and she rushed upstairs to shower. She thought I didn't notice what she was doing. So fast forward, McCall asked me to stay after class today, and I smelled the same damn scent from Jessica's neck! He told me that it was his cologne."

Kristen was completely overwhelmed. The same thing that she tried to keep her best friend from, she ran to with open arms. There was no taking it back; it was all over. What the two of them had to figure out was if they were going to report what they just found out.

"Brandon, this is a lot! I really don't know what to do."

"Jessica expects me to move past it, but I'm not about to let this man walk free. After Jessica, someone else will be next."

Kristen looked at her phone and saw that she had back-to-back messages from Jessica.

"It's Jess."

"I don't even have anything to say to her right now."

"Brandon, I don't know if I feel comfortable with going to Mr. Martin or Miss Robin about all of this."

"Yeah, I know what you mean. Maybe we should find someone at school to further this information to. We need someone trustworthy."

"He's Principal Chutney's friend; nobody is going to believe us."

Brandon knew that Kristen made some valid points, but that was not going to stop him from doing what was right. He knew that there was someone at the school who felt the same way about Derrick McCall, and it was time to bring all of this to their attention. Kristen agreed to go with Brandon to speak about everything that transpired, but they all knew that none of this would be completely resolved if Jessica did not speak up.

The next day, Kristen tried her best to keep quiet until she and Brandon went to speak to Mrs. Thompson. Everyone knew that Mrs. Thompson did not trust Mr. McCall. She had a special place in her heart for these students, and their safety was her top priority. Both

Brandon and Kristen waited until after school to go to the guidance office. They sat in the conference room with Mrs. Thompson thinking about what was about to occur.

"So, what's going on guys?"

"There's a possibility that Mr. McCall has been closer to Jessica than a teacher should."

"And how do you know this?"

"I smelled his cologne on her neck a couple of weeks ago."

Mrs. Thompson knew that this evidence was minimal, but she knew that Brandon was indeed telling the truth. She didn't trust McCall, but she needed more evidence.

"That is one piece of evidence, but before I can do anything, I need more. I'm almost certain that Jessica is not going to speak up, at least not right now. However, I can assure you that I am going to do whatever I can to get more evidence. I also need to contact her parents."

Mrs. Thompson had a lot on her plate. She was going to do what she had to do and get rid of Derrick McCall. She had a few connections at the hotel where the yearbook staff stayed when they were in San Antonio. It was time to get with them and review security cameras and some other things. Whatever she was about to do, she had to act on it quickly.

"Thank you for coming by. Are you hungry?"

"It's late, and I already had dinner."

"A lot is going on and I think we should be on the same page just in case things start to get out of hand."

"What you're saying is, you want me to cover your ass."

Derrick asked Jessica to stop by in the middle of the night. She couldn't believe that she went over to his house, but she had already told her mother that she was staying at Kristen's house for the night. Her plan was to tell Mr. McCall to stay out of her way and that she wanted to move on from this big mistake. Likewise, Mr. McCall had his own agenda for the night."

"Jessica, you can relax. Nobody is coming by here at this time of night."

"I just came by to tell you that what we had going on was a big mistake, and let's just forget that it all happened."

"Just like that?"

"Yep."

"Jessica, we both know how mature you are for your age."

"That still does not justify me sleeping with you."

"Are you afraid that your High School boyfriend will find out? You and I know that you deserve someone like me." Derrick began kissing on Jessica's neck.

"It's illegal!"

"The same way it was illegal when your panties hit the floor back in San Antonio. It was all fair game then."

Jessica knew what Derrick was trying to do, but she was not giving in. It was time for her to focus. She could pretty much get into any college of her choice, and she could not allow anything or anyone get in the way of her promising future.

"We both know that we have a lot on the line. So let's move on and silence all of this noise."

"One last time."

"What?"

"You let me have you one last time and then we can move on."

"Are you threatening me?"

"You and I know that we don't need to take it there. Just as I want to free you of those clothes, you want to go up to my room."

Jessica messed up. She was feeling weak and vulnerable and McCall could see that. He led Jessica up to his dark bedroom and placed her on his California King Bed. Jackpot! If McCall could score tonight, she was his forever. Slow motion, loud noises, and strong grips. For the time being, all of Jessica's worries were gone. His body was against hers, their legs intertwined, and Derrick used his left hand to knock down the photo of him and Lisa that was placed on his nightstand.

# CHAPTER 7

# HIDDEN SECRETS

It had been a couple of days since Lisa showed up at Robin's office. Robin hadn't spoken to Martin about the conversation that she and Lisa had because she was too upset. She needed a few days to herself to actually think about what she was going to say when she decided to have a sit-down conversation with him. Robin did not want to yell or scream, but she was certainly going to get her point across. Robin invited Martin over, and she knew that Lisa had more than likely given her side of the story by now. At this point, she did not care. She was going to get to the bottom of the entire situation.

"Hey Robin."

"Hey. Thanks for coming over and agreeing to talk to me."

"Sure. I'm curious to know what the hell I did wrong now."

"Why does everything have to be like this whenever we get around each other?"

Things were going well during the counseling sessions, but Martin and Robin couldn't keep it together once they left the office.

"I don't cause the tension, you do."

"How so?"

"Robin, every time we are together you are always yelling and screaming for no apparent reason."

"I'll take the blame on that, but that is because you keep placing me into these stupid situations."

"Like what?"

"Like your girlfriend showing up at my job with a check to buy my share of your business."

Martin had a confused look on his face as if he did not know what Robin was referring to. Martin and Lisa hadn't seen much of one another in the past few days. One thing Martin did not do was discuss his business affairs with Lisa. He just didn't think that they were at that point in their relationship. Each time that Lisa would imply that she wanted to become more hands-on with Martin's business affairs, Martin would gently end the conversation altogether.

"Robin where is all of this coming from? What happened?"

"It's been about a week now since Lisa decided that she would come into my office with a down payment to purchase my share of the business."

"Say what?"

"You mean to tell me that you sleep with this woman every night, and you have no idea about the stunts that she's been trying to pull since day one?"

"Stunts?"

"Let's be clear Martin; I don't have a problem with your girlfriend. She has her personal issues with me for no apparent reason. What I do know is that she needs to understand that we have a business partnership. We both have worked too hard to build what we have done so far. The relationship didn't work, but so be it. We still have a daughter to look out for and we still have business to take care of. So your girlfriend needs to sit in the bleachers until I see an engagement and a marriage take place."

One thing Robin could do was handle business and Martin loved it! He was so turned on by his ex-wife's demeanor. He missed all of that now that they were divorced, and he was clearly not seeing those characteristics in Lisa. Not to be mistaken, Lisa was a great woman, but Martin wasn't too sure that she was the right woman for him.

"Robin, to be honest, I haven't seen much of Lisa these past few days."

"Really? Where's she been? At her brother's house plotting more business propositions?"

"Brother?"

"Her brother. The check that Lisa gave to me was from her brother, Derrick McCall. He wrote the check, signed it and everything."

"Robin, Lisa doesn't have any brothers. She has one sister out in Atlanta that I met a couple of times."

"Well, that is what I was told. Lisa handed me the check and I saw his name on the top. I then asked who Derrick McCall was and she said that he was her brother. Then, I ripped the check up."

Martin couldn't believe what he was hearing, but he needed to get some answers from Lisa and maybe even Derrick. Truthfully, he was embarrassed, but he did not want Robin to know that. Despite all of the resentment that Robin had towards her ex-husband, he was still her friend. She knew that Martin loved Lisa and he was truly committed to their relationship. In fact, it used to hurt Robin to see Martin love another woman. She was learning to accept all of the changes that were made over the years, but it was a very emotional time for their family. At the end of the day, these two were always going to look out for one another. They were a team for the past 20 years and it was pretty clear that the game wasn't over yet.

Mrs. Thompson spent her weekend in San Antonio gathering some much-needed information about these allegations. She wanted to solidify every accusation that Brandon and Kristen placed on Mr. McCall, but she had already made up her mind of what she believed to be true. While she didn't let the students know about what she was doing in San Antonio, or about any other further investigation that she was going to make, she assured them that their friend would be supported and taken care of.

"I need to talk to you."

"Angela, I have a busy afternoon. Unless the school is on fire, could you just notify me later?"

"I think you better take your eyes off of that computer screen and listen to what I have to say."

Principal Chutney and Mrs. Thompson have known each other for quite some time. About 15 years ago, the two of them were engaged, but the relationship did not follow through. Honestly, Mrs. Thompson knew that Chutney wanted things to turn out differently, but it was time to leave the past where it was. They were colleagues now and it was time to get the job done under any circumstances. Moments later, Principal Chutney followed Mrs. Thompson into the conference room. He was greeted by Officer Kingston, the school's Liaison, and a young lady that he did not know. She looked to be about 23 years old.

"Good afternoon everybody. Uh, Mrs. Thompson, what's going on?"

"A couple of days ago some students brought to my attention that there was a teacher who could be having sexual relations with a student."

Principal Chutney dropped down in his chair. He would never have imagined that he would be dealing with such a serious situation.

"How could something like this happen in my school and I was not informed? Officer Kingston, you always find out everything about these kids. If it were true, you would have known, right?"

"Hidden secrets," Officer Kingston shrugged.

"I knew that when it happened to me that my Principal would be in denial too. That's why I never said anything, but I wish I would have."

"And who might you be young lady?"

"Principal Chutney, meet Olivia Sollers. Olivia works at the hotel where we stayed for the yearbook conference. She's good friends with my nephew who is a manager there."

"I'm confused."

"When two of our students mentioned to me that they knew a teacher was sleeping with their friend, I called my nephew to check their security tapes."

"So Miss Olivia, where do you come into play?"

"I was a student who never spoke up when this teacher did the same thing to me."

Chutney put the pieces together once Mrs. Thompson mentioned something about the conference.

"What student and teacher are we referring to?"

"Jessica DeLaney and Derrick McCall."

Chutney was completely heartbroken! This man was his best friend, his little brother. McCall got his job by Principal Chutney making a few phone calls, and this was about to cause more problems. Mrs. Thompson called Martin and Robin to ask them to join in on this meeting as soon as possible. While they waited on their arrival, Principal Chutney had Derrick come to his office.

"What's up, boss?"

"That's what I'm trying to figure out."

"Huh?" Derrick tried to act as if he didn't know what Martin was referring to.

"I got heat in the conference room, man! They have proof that you have been sleeping with Jessica DeLaney. A student!"

"Come on, Chut. You're going to believe a kid who probably just has a little high school crush?"

"I saw the video."

"What video?"

"Got a hold of the video of you and her entering the same hotel room back in San Antonio. Spare me the details."

Derrick couldn't believe what he was hearing. He knew that Jessica must have said something to someone, but maybe the video part was a lie. Maybe they were just trying to get him to admit to the whole thing.

"It's her word against mine."

"Wrong! It's yours, hers, and Olivia's. I have to talk to her parents and I'm sending a substitute to cover your classes. They're going to come get you momentarily for some questioning. For now, just cool it in here."

Derrick was still puzzled from Principal Chutney mentioning Olivia's name. Olivia was a student at McCall's previous high school. She never really felt as if she was attracted to Derrick, but somehow she continued to sleep with him for a few months. It was extremely difficult for Olivia to speak about this situation to anyone, and when she found out the latest situation at hand, she knew that she had to share her side of the story. Principal Chutney had sweat everywhere on his body! He was about to meet the DeLaney family and Martin was already prepared to raise hell. Mrs. Thompson had just explained to both Robin and Martin the reason why they were called in for a meeting.

"What the hell are you trying to tell me right now? There is no way that my baby girl has been sleeping with some punk ass English teacher!"

"Where is he? I know he isn't still in this building." Robin scolded.

"Uh, allow me to interrupt if I could. Mr. and Ms. DeLaney, I know we have only spoken briefly over the past few years, but I wish we could have met under better circumstances."

"How could you be so blind to what's going on in this school?"

"In his defense, just as soon as the situation was brought to our attention, proper action was taken."

"Why the hell are we just being notified?" Robin cried.

"Give me his name! I want a damn name!"

"Mr. DeLaney, I can assure you that the law enforcement is doing everything so that justice is served. Taking matters into your own hands could stir up a lot more trouble."

"Did he fuck your daughter?"

"No sir, he did not."

"Then don't give me any false hopes!"

Olivia was getting emotional as she listened to Martin express his feelings. She knew that her father would have reacted the same way if she would have told someone back when she was in Jessica's position. They called Jessica to the conference room moments later and she just about had a heart attack when she saw everyone. First, Mrs. Thompson and Principal Chutney took Jessica into a private office for a quick moment. They wanted to see if they could get her to open up more without her parents around.

"They know, don't they? The whole school probably knows by now."

"The question is, why didn't we know? Jessica, since your freshman year here at Lenwood, I have made it very clear that you all could come to me whenever something was going wrong. I am here to support you. You are one of our brightest students, and I really expected more."

"It's not like I planned for any of this to happen."

"Are you saying that Mr. McCall forced you to do it?"

"Like rape? No! Mr. McCall's just manipulative. He has a way of making you say yes when you don't want to."

"Is that what happened in San Antonio?"

"Can I please talk about this another time? I really want to get back to class."

"Miss DeLaney, I think it's best if you don't go back to class. Your parents agreed that you should go home with them for the remainder of the day."

Jessica had never been in any hot water with her parents. She wasn't perfect, but she had her priorities together, at least she once did. Robin was completely in tears and Martin was at a loss for words.

"Mr. DeLaney, Ms. DeLaney, I can assure you that Mr. Derrick McCall will not be back in this school without this situation being resolved."

"What name did you just say?"

"Derrick McCall. That's the teacher's name."

Robin and Martin followed Jessica back to the house. Jessica's heart was pounding! The cell-phone that Derrick had given her was vibrating, but she knew better than to answer it.

"I'm going to let your mother talk because I can't even gather my thoughts."

"Daddy, do you hate me?"

"I could never hate you, but I hate this! I HATE THIS! You have allowed yourself to get involved with a teacher and you said nothing! You did exactly what Olivia did."

"Who's Olivia?"

"Olivia was the young lady in the conference room."

"Why was she there?"

"She was there as an advocate for you. Apparently, this Mr. McCall was involved with her when she was in high school some years back.

She never told anyone. She just kept it to herself. Jessica, go up to your room. I need to speak to your father."

Jessica felt as if she was just another target on McCall's list. He had promised her that she was the only girl that he had feelings for. This all became a nightmare.

"You need to call Lisa."

"I ain't thinking about Lisa right now. What I'm concerned about is what I'm going to do to this jackass if I find out they don't keep him in custody."

"Did you not pay attention when they said that Derrick McCall was this teacher's name?"

This made Martin irate! He couldn't handle the fact that the woman he's been in a relationship with could possibly be a part of this painful situation.

"You get her over here and I'm talking right now!"

At the sound of the dismissal bell, Lisa saw that she had a lot of missed calls from Martin.

"I knew he'd come to his senses," Lisa smiled.

She thought that he had finally gotten Robin to sell her share of the business, but she did not want to jump to any conclusions. She hurried and grabbed her belongings so that she could call Martin. Lisa was in such a hurry that she didn't even notice that Derrick's classroom was completely dark.

"Hello."

"Hey, I saw that I missed a few of your calls."

"Yeah. Lisa, we need to talk like right now."

"Ok. Well, I'll be at the house in about 15 minutes. I'm just about to leave the school."

"Actually, could you meet me over at Robin's house? You remember where she lives?"

"Ok, yeah. I'm headed over there now. Just give me about 10 minutes."

As far as Lisa was concerned, this was all working out in her favor. She thought that she was about to walk into Robin's house and negotiate this business deal, but she was so wrong.

"Hello, Robin."

"Come in, Lisa."

"Thank you. This is such a lovely home."

On the way over, Lisa decided that she was going to be pleasant to Robin because she did not want anything to interfere with her gaining 50% of the business.

"Lisa, there's been a lot going on lately, and you've been involved in all of it as far as I'm concerned."

"Excuse me?"

"Let's start by talking about the check that you gave me without Martin even knowing."

"Yeah. I'm waiting to hear about this. Lisa, we've never talked about you gaining partnership of the business."

"I'm the woman in your life now, right?"

"Some days."

"What?"

"You show up at the house when you want to, and then I find out that you're pulling these stunts behind my back! Come on, Lisa!"

"Ok enough! You are not going to sit here and act as if I'm the one being unfaithful when you're over here 24/7. I guess you're getting re-acquainted with your old bed."

"Lisa don't come up in my house talking all of that nonsense just to justify what you have been doing all along!"

"I've been working."

Jessica was sitting in the stairway witnessing what was going on, and she felt as if she was the blame. She knew that everything involving Derrick was about to be revealed, but she did not know how Lisa was connected to the situation. She knew that Lisa had been around McCall quite a few times, but maybe it was just a friendship.

"Lisa, the "brother" that wrote me that check, he's in a lot of hot water with me, with Martin, and with the legal system. But Martin told me that you don't even have a brother!"

"Why does that matter? The check will clear. What the hell do you mean he's in hot water?"

Lisa thought she was there to handle business. She was not about to reveal how she was affiliated with Derrick, and Jessica was not going to talk about her seeing Lisa over at Derrick's house.

"It matters because this damn man has been sleeping with my 17-year-old daughter!" Martin cried.

The situation at hand was very emotional for Martin. He felt as if his daughter had been taken advantage of and it did not sit right on his heart. Lisa could not grasp what she was witnessing. Her heart was aching, but she was not going to let her emotions show. Despite how she felt about Robin or where her relationship was going with Martin, she felt pain for the entire family.

"These kind of accusations are really serious. There are lives and reputations on the line." Lisa warned.

"Are you defending this coward?"

"He's no coward! This man is my husband. My ex-husband."

Lisa decided that she had said enough. She walked out of the house and Robin's mouth dropped. She was overwhelmed by all of the drama. Martin was heartbroken even more now. This was his first serious relationship since he had gotten divorced. Prior to all of this chaos, Lisa had shown Martin that she was ready to build a solid foundation, but now all of that had changed. It was now time for him to set the relationship aside and make sure that his daughter was protected at all times.

"Wow. I can't believe she lied to you, Martin."

"Forget all of that. I'll handle that situation. We need to further this conversation with Jessica."

Robin and Martin did have the chance to watch the security tape from the hotel in San Antonio. Now, each time they saw Jessica, they just saw her walking into that hotel room, giving away her respect, her class, her beauty. The fact that she agreed to have sex with Derrick McCall tore them apart.

"Jessica, you've had a few hours to get yourself together, and now it's time to talk to me and your father."

Jessica was curled up in her bed. For the first time in months, she looked like a 17-year-old girl should look. Robin recalled how her daughter was starting to be a bit more mature. She even thought about the lingerie that she saw her daughter wearing in the tape.

"I'm sorry. I'm so, so sorry." Jessica cried.

"Jess, baby girl, sorry doesn't work. You wanted to be an adult, deal with an adult, and now it's time to own up to what you have done."

Jessica felt like she was being attacked by her father, and she needed his love and support now more than ever. Typically, both Robin and Martin would come to Jessica's rescue, but today they had to let her vouch for herself.

"I didn't want to get involved with Mr. McCall, really I didn't. It just happened."

"Things like this don't just happen!"

"He kept coming towards me. He was in my face at the basketball game, the Winter Formal, and then he became the yearbook sponsor just to be around me."

"Did you think that sleeping with him would keep him away?"

"No! Maybe. I don't know."

"Was San Antonio the only time that you had sex with Mr. Mc-Call?"

Jessica began to burst out into tears. She could not prepare herself to tell her parents the truth about her relations with Mr. McCall. She didn't want any more anger to show. Her mother was an emotional wreck and her father was pacing back and forth, just waiting to explode.

"We had sex in his bedroom."

Martin slammed Jessica's door and ran downstairs.

"Jess!"

"I'm sorry."

"Do you realize that you could have been killed?!"

"I was wrong."

"Absolutely. You absolutely were wrong."

Robin had a lot of emotions arousing, but she had to rid some of the tension that was in her home.

"DeLaney."

"Not now, Robin."

"If not now, then when?"

"She's up there giving us all of these damn details like we're one of her little girlfriends."

"It's better we know now than to wait until we get into the courtroom."

"I can't take it!"

"And I can? You really think that I want to go through this? All of this? Ain't nobody holding my hand! I'm down here consoling you, I'm up there trying to comfort our daughter despite what she did, and ain't nobody there for me. I need somebody too! What about me?"

# CHAPTER 8

# THE TWO DO NOT COMPARE

Jessica had been doing her schoolwork from home for the past few days. She hadn't seen or talked to anyone besides her parents and the lawyer. Mrs. Thompson had been reaching out to Martin and Robin to make sure that Jessica was continuing to do well with her studies. The dynamics of her life had changed, and she had to learn how to adapt. Jessica was returning to school later that week, but she wanted to meet with Mrs. Thompson and make sure that she would go back to as much normalcy as possible.

"Jessica, we're extremely proud of you for returning to finish out the school year."

"At least it's almost over," Jessica added.

"At the request of your parents, we have adjusted your schedule so that you are with Mrs. Campbell for English."

"Ok."

Jessica just wanted to be as cooperative as possible. She did not mind the schedule change, especially since she and Kristen hadn't been speaking as much. Honestly, she missed her best friend, but so much was changing right before her very eyes.

"Unfortunately, there were some things that we had to discontinue."

"Like what?"

"We're going to have to discontinue your time as the yearbook editor."

Jessica froze! She could not believe that all of the things that she had worked so hard for were being taken away from her.

"If that's what you all think is best."

"In doing what's best, we think that you should not become captain of the cheerleading squad next year."

"WHAT?"

This was enough to break Jessica's now fragile heart. She worked so hard to get to this position that she was in as far as her extracurricular activities went. The yearbook was a major part of her life, but she had a different kind of love for cheerleading. Since Jessica was a toddler, she had been on competitive cheerleading teams. Her parents would travel with her and support her through every competition and every practice. This was all being disregarded at this moment as far as Jessica was concerned.

"This can't be! I've worked way too hard to hold this team together. You can't take this from me! I'm sorry... I own up to my mistakes... Just please don't do this."

"We're not taking you off of the team. We're just making the changes that we feel are necessary to change the focal point."

"Basically, you don't want the parents to keep talking about the "fast ass" cheerleader that slept with her teacher."

"This benefits you. Now Jessica, I support you, but you have to accept the consequences for your actions."

Jessica was starting to feel as if everyone was turning against her. Things were starting to go downhill and everything that Jessica had worked so hard for was beginning to disappear. She just wanted to disconnect from reality, but it was time for her to face the music.

"Everything that I've worked so hard for at this school is being taken from me. This school is not even standing behind me."

"Then speak up!"

Jessica walked out of the guidance office and met her mother in the front parking lot.

"Jess, what did you think the consequences would be for you sleeping with your teacher?"

"I didn't think anyone would find out."

"Say what? So you thought you could just sweep this under the rug?"

"I said I was sorry!"

"Baby, you can't expect anyone else to accept your apology until you accept it for yourself."

Jessica thought about what her mother had said the entire ride home. This was all starting to get overwhelming, and she was unsure if she was ready to return to Lenwood High School. Tomorrow she would have to face judgmental people, and she knew that she would not have her two closest friends around her for support. Jessica and Kristen hadn't seen each other or talked to one another in the past few weeks.

Kristen didn't regret telling Mrs. Thompson about Jessica and Mr. McCall, but she missed her best friend. Jessica wasn't completely convinced that Kristen went to Mrs. Thompson along with Brandon, but she had an idea. At this point, Jessica just wanted to stay home for a few more weeks, but that was beyond her control.

"Mom, why are we going this way?"

"Going to lunch."

"Lunch? Mom, I'm not hungry. Can I just go home and take a nap?"

"Not yet. I promised someone that we would meet them for lunch."

Jessica was done with being surprised. She just wanted to get home and sleep her pain away. She didn't want to be around anyone. This situation had really taken a toll on her and the way she was dealing with everything going on in her life. Jessica had been wearing jogging suits and tennis shoes just about every day. She was hiding in her room as well as hiding in her clothes. Mr. McCall would constantly compliment Jessica's various body parts. He would slowly caress her shoulders and kiss her on her collar bone. It made Jessica feel so uncomfortable, but sometimes she felt happy to have someone craving her so deeply. Jessica was beginning to miss the attention, but she did not miss Mr. McCall.

When Robin and Jessica arrived at the restaurant, they joined Olivia at the table.

"Hello, hello. Jess, you remember Olivia, right?"

"Yeah I do. Hi, Olivia."

"Hey. How are you doing?"

"I'm doing ok."

Just when Jessica thought that she was done with dealing with this situation, her mother sets up a lunch date with Olivia. She didn't really get the chance to get to know Olivia on a personal level; she just knew that she too slept with Mr. McCall.

"Jessica, I know that it may have been a very rough situation a couple of weeks ago in the conference room. I'm sure having me there unexpectedly did not help the situation. Even though you don't know me, trust me when I say that I was there to support you wholeheartedly. That's why I got in contact with your mother to assure you that I would be willing to testify against Derrick in court."

Jessica did not like confrontation. She never thought that she was actually going to take this in front of a judge. All she wanted to do was transfer to a different High School and then move away for college. Now she was forced to deal with everything that was going on.

"Court?"

"Your mom said that you all are taking this to court."

"We are."

"I just don't want to make a big deal."

"I can understand because I felt the same way some years ago, but believe me when I say that you have to say something! You have to speak up!"

"I consented."

"You are a child; he's an adult! The two do not compare." Robin interrupted.

Robin didn't speak much, but it frustrated her to think that her daughter was trying to protect Mr. McCall. Jessica knew that by testifying it would allow her and Olivia to speak their truth. It was a part of the healing process and the only way that she could finally move on. Olivia was a good supporter and she was starting to become the sister that Jessica had always wanted. It took her a while to even look at Derrick McCall, and she knew that it would most likely be the same for

Jessica. Martin hadn't seen or talked to Jessica and Robin in the past few days. He was dealing with a lot of emotions, and Robin felt as if he was being selfish. Lisa had yet to come back to the house to gather her things, and Martin wasn't sure of what would happen when she finally did return. All of a sudden, he heard keys rattling in the doorknob.

"Oh! I didn't think you would be home. I figured you would be over at Robin's house or something."

"No. I'm here."

"I just came to grab my stuff."

"Is that what it's come to? You sneaking to get your things? You not telling me that you are still a married woman?"

"You want to talk about secrets, Martin? What about you sneaking off to your ex-wife's house damn near every night?"

"To check on my daughter!"

"Your daughter is damn near grown, and if she isn't grown then she shouldn't be sleeping with grown ass men!"

"What the hell did you just say? Lisa, you better get out of my house. I will pack up all of your shit and you can come get it later."

Lisa slammed the door. Martin wanted to punch a hole in the wall. He did not recognize the woman that had just left his home not too long ago. There wasn't an emotion that he hadn't felt in the past few weeks. His daughter had been putting herself in certain situations that could have been life-threatening. It hurt him so much. As to be expected, it seemed as if Robin was numb to pain after dealing with everything that they had been through in the past few years. They all struggled with handling their emotions properly. Martin hadn't been by the house lately, but he knew that he had to check and see how the legal affairs were being handled.

"Hey, Martin."

"Whoa, whoa, whoa."

"What?"

"You must not be angry with me today."

"What are you talking about?"

"Normally, ever since we divorced, you'd call me DeLaney. You called me Martin just now." He grinned.

"Big deal," Robin laughed.

"I'm winning my friend back."

"Stop acting like I've treated you badly lately."

"You have, but no hard feelings. Where's Jess?"

"Sleep."

"She nervous about going back to school?"

"I'm sure, but it's time. It's best that she continues with her life as best as she can."

"As mad as I want to be, that is still my baby girl."

"Martin, I'm not trying to be tough, I'm just trying to protect her before anything else happens."

"I agree, but we can't protect her forever. All of the medical examinations turned out good, right?"

"Yes, thank God."

"Look, I'll come by tomorrow morning. Are you driving her to school?"

"I'm letting her drive. I just want to keep some sort of normalcy around here."

"I'll come by before she leaves."

"Goodnight... Delaney." Robin laughed.

"Derrick, Derrick!"

Lisa walked into Derrick's house around 5 AM.

"What's up?"

"I'm trying to keep your daily routine the same."

"I don't have anything to do."

"So what! The bail wasn't posted for you to just hide out. Your reputation is on the line!"

"Don't you think I know that? Look, I have a lot going on, and I don't need any pressure."

"I'm not trying to pressure you, but I am your wife."

"So now you want to play the marriage game?" After you slept around and flaunted all you had, now you want to play "For better or for worse?"

Derrick was deeply in love with Lisa, and when the two of them thought that they were divorcing, he searched for a piece of her in any female that he came in contact with.

"I believe in you. I support you. Derrick, I want your name cleared! We have been through so much, but I could never walk away."

"We both walked away when we thought we filed for divorce."

"Let that go! If you can do that, then I can come back to my husband."

"What about coming back to bed with your husband?"

Derrick grabbed Lisa closer and started kissing her on the neck.

"You smell radiant for it only being 5 AM."

"Let's not do this."

"Lisa, baby, please come to bed."

"As long as there are no teenage girls in your bed."

"Never that."

Derrick couldn't wait to make love to his wife! Lisa was finally giving her all, but she didn't know the complete truth about Derrick and what's been going on during the time of their marriage. She couldn't deny that sex with Derrick was beyond amazing, and even better because she was married to him. He took her to a place that no man ever could. She loved being in love with Derrick, and she planned to show him any way she could.

"We can't just sit home and have sex all day."

"We're not. We're going to make breakfast, you're going to work, and I'll be waiting for round two when you get home."

"Have you spoken to your lawyer?"

"Yeah."

"Well?"

"Well... He's not even sure that Jessica will talk."

"It doesn't matter! Her parents aren't just going to let her stay silent. I know."

"That's right. You know them very well, her father especially."

"Derrick we have to be prepared to fight!"

"You have to be prepared to let me handle this."

Lisa had a problem with minding her own business. Truthfully, this was her business, and she did not want to see her husband behind bars. It was a lot on her when Derrick was taken into custody for the two days until the bail was posted. She knew that she had a few conversations to have, and she knew that she had to act quickly. Lisa hated going behind her husband's back, but she had to do it.

"Good Morning."

"Morning."

"Jessica ready?"

"She's in the kitchen."

"What's wrong with you?"

"I just really want Jessica to have a good day."

"Martin, we have to let her gain some independence back. Not too much, but we have to slowly show her that we trust her."

"I just want her to be able to focus on her school work."

"That she will."

Jessica walked into the family room and grabbed her keys. She was wearing a pair of ripped jeans and a sweatshirt. Her hair was freshly washed, and she placed it into a high bun. There was no sign of make-up and she wore her glasses instead of her contacts.

"Morning, Jessica."

"Morning, Daddy."

"I just wanted to make sure that you have a good day."

"Thanks."

"Have a good day, baby."

"I'll be home after school."

Jessica walked outside and drove off to Lenwood High School. She drove in silence instead of listening to her favorite morning radio show. Jessica was thinking about how she wouldn't have to sit in English class by her friend that she hadn't spoken to in a while, and she now didn't have to revisit the memories of Mr. McCall standing up in that same room, doing anything to get her attention.

"My daughter hates me."

"What are you talking about?"

"Jessica's been ignoring me ever since she found out that we're pressing charges."

"She's never been the one to like confrontation."

"Maybe we should have respected her wishes."

"She's a child! Come on, Robin. You know that we are doing what's best for our daughter. In the end, she will be taken care of and that's why this is my main focus. We just have to stick to the plan."

"That's easy for you to say because you're used to her being mad at you." Robin laughed.

"I'll be the bad guy with no problem. But I know that as long as my daughter is good, then I'm fighting a battle that's worth it. My job is to protect her until the day I die."

The minute that Jessica parked her car, she noticed so many people staring at her. Typically, Jessica was one of the most popular students in school for all of the right reasons, but lately, she had been gaining some unwanted attention.

"Hey Jessica."

"Jess, hey."

"Hey."

High School was a bit confusing for some. The students were either trying to befriend Jessica to get more information, or the guys felt that since she had been sleeping with a teacher, they now had a fair chance.

"Good Morning, students. Today I want to start showing you a film that will take us into the weekend. Please pay attention because there will be a test and a project on this film upon your return. Once again, please pay attention."

Jessica had been out of school for two weeks and she was so glad to be watching a movie during English class. Jessica sat at the desk right by the door. The minute that the bell sounded, Jessica had planned to be out of the classroom. Kristen couldn't believe that Jessica hadn't spoken to her all day. She wasn't even aware that Jessica was coming back to Lenwood. Their friendship had really been tested in the past few weeks, and Kristen knew that she was going to have to speak with Jessica and let her know how she was feeling. When the bell rang, Jessica ran straight out of the door and headed towards her locker. Kristen thought about ignoring her friend, but she wasn't the type of person who could just ignore a problem.

"Hey, Jess."

"Hey."

"Are you ok?"

"I'm fine. Why?"

"Well, you seem a bit upset."

"How would you feel coming back here after everything that went on?"

"I don't know, but I do know that you are not being fair to your friends and family that care. We are here to support you, but we can't do that if you keep pushing everybody away."

Jessica knew that Kristen was telling her everything that she needed to hear. Yes, Jessica was a child, but she was old enough to know that sleeping with the English teacher on multiple occasions was wrong! Nevertheless, Jessica had a great number of people supporting her, and it was time for her to appreciate that. Mrs. Thompson knew that she wasn't one of Jessica's favorite people right now, but she wanted to see her student move on with the best life she could.

"Jessica."

"Yes?"

"Could I see you in my office for a quick second?"

"Ok."

Jessica was sick and tired of sitting in people's offices. She had been sitting and had been getting questioned for the past few weeks. Coincidentally, her answers were all becoming repetitive.

"No, he didn't rape me."

That was all Jessica continued to say. She wasn't trying to save Mr. McCall, but she did not want things to continue to escalate the way that they were. At this point, Mrs. Thompson knew everything that Jessica knew. This was the reason why Jessica couldn't think of a reason that Mrs. Thompson still wanted to constantly speak with her every day.

"How was your first day back?"

"It was fine."

"Are you getting readjusted?"

"I am."

"Good, good. Look, Jessica, since you've been here at Lenwood, I have tried to make it clear that I am always here for you whenever you need me. If I can help with anything for any student, I am always willing to do so."

"I'm moving on from all of this. I have accepted that I have made mistakes and I am willing to handle the consequences."

Jessica was trying to tell Mrs. Thompson in the nicest way that she was done with the entire situation. She was ready to focus on life after High School at this point. Jessica had a lot that she wanted to accomplish and this could possibly end all of her plans.

"Sounds to me as if you're placing all of the blame on yourself."

"I never said that."

"I apologize for making an assumption. I was wrong for that."

"Can we catch up another time? I have to be home right after school."

"Of course. Thank you for your time."

Jessica grabbed her things and headed towards the parking lot. She had decided that she was no longer going to give out any more information to anyone. She wanted to just move forward in a peaceful way. On the drive home, Jessica just turned the radio off. She had an overwhelming first day back and she knew that Robin would want to know just about every detail of her day. Jessica just wanted to take a nap! She had one thing that she really needed to do. She needed to give Derrick McCall his phone back. Jessica was tempted to take it face-to-face, but she knew how big that risk would be. Oddly enough, McCall went to San Antonio. Word had gotten around that Olivia had planned on testifying against him on Jessica's behalf, and he wanted to see if he could charm her out of the original plan.

"Oh no."

"Hey, Olivia. It's been a long time."

"What do you want?"

"I want to just sincerely apologize for everything that went on in the past."

"That's the past."

"If you've let go of the past, how come you're so adamant about these pending charges I have. You stayed quiet for seven years, and now you have something to say?"

"Don't you dare! You are a sick, twisted individual. You think I'm going to let that little girl suffer the way that I did?"

Olivia had so many different emotions built up inside of her. She couldn't believe what was happening. All of these years she's been running from her demons, and today they were staring at her right in the face.

"Look, I can only offer my apologies. It is clear that we have both moved on from the entire situation and I just think that we should not revisit the past any longer."

"Get out. Get out!"

Olivia ran to the staff lounge. She was starting to revisit a dark, evil place that she never wanted to see again. Derrick knew that she was going to talk in court, and she was going to tell everything that she could. He couldn't stop this one. A few days later, Derrick had a package on his front step with no return address. When he opened it, there was the phone that he had given Jessica, and there was a note attached.

***"You,***

***This was the last and final thing that I had that belonged to you. I wish I didn't even have that phone. My life is now a complete mess and it's all because my teacher couldn't just teach the class. He had to look at me in the most devastating ways, and then he had his way with me. Now, I'm taking back my life, you can't have that!"***

This was just the way that Derrick wanted to end his day. He now realized that he had created a whirlwind of trouble. If he could take it all back, he would in a heartbeat, but he knew that the damage was already done. Derrick slammed the phone down in anger and stomped on it until there were micro pieces. He was screaming and crying heavily, and everything was now out in the open. His career was now in jeopardy, and he was unsure as to how he would survive from here on out. He hurried and cleaned up the remains of the phone because he knew that Lisa would be home soon. Lisa was out doing anything in her power to clear her husband's name. Even when the two of them were no longer together, she still did whatever she could for Derrick because legally, she was still married.

"Chutney, thanks for agreeing to meet with me."

"I came to check on Derrick. Right or wrong, that's been my friend for years, but as a parent, this hits home."

"You think that Derrick did it?"

"I don't want to place the blame. I want to separate business from personal, and I want to believe that my friend stands on the morals and values that I know he believes in."

"We have to defend him!"

"No. We have to support him! We have to encourage him to do right, but we don't have to defend anything that we may not fully understand."

"Is she going to be taking any responsibility for her part?"

"She's a child!"

"She knew!"

"Why are you so against this girl?"

"I'm not."

Principal Chutney had known Lisa for years! He remembered exactly when she and Derrick began their relationship. By being around her for so long, he knew when Lisa was feeling a certain way about something. She was like a sister to him. That meant a few different things – He would always love and support her and he would always tell her his opinion on something.

"Have you called him, Chut? Have you gone to talk to him?"

"No I haven't."

"Well, you should. He's losing faith. He's acting like he doesn't have a voice in this. He's acting as if he's given up!"

Chutney was in a very difficult position; As Principal of Lenwood High, he wanted to support his best friend and support him no matter the outcome. However, it was his job to support his staff and student body as well.

"He's not giving up."

"How would you know if you haven't even reached out to him?"

"He needs his space."

"No! He doesn't need space. He needs his friends and loved ones sticking behind him."

"Is he denying it?"

"What?"

"Is he denying the allegations?"

"Chut, for as long as I have known Derrick, the two of you have been side-by-side. You have been there for him, and he has been there for you! Are you really telling me that you can't back your brother up?"

Chutney and Derrick had a 25-year friendship. They grew up playing on the same sports teams and they went to school together. Over the years, they have turned their friendship into a brotherhood. Their families were close, and they were each other's best man at their weddings. Things have gotten a bit out of hand since the accusations came about. To be honest, Chutney believed that Derrick did indeed sleep with Jessica. For the record, he did not know prior to all of this happening, but he did know that he had to do the right thing as a man, as a father, and as a Principal.

"Lisa, Derrick is and will always be my brother. We have been there for one another, but this has gotten to be quite the situation."

"He needs you!"

"I needed him! I needed him to be a strong, black teacher! I needed him to teach the students, not sleep with them. I needed him to be somebody these kids could respect and look up to. I needed him just that much."

# CHAPTER 9

# ONE LAST TIME

Jessica was now starting to get back into her normal school routine. She was studying for final exams and preparing to go to trial all within a couple of weeks. There were still a lot of emotions that she was dealing with, but things were beginning to look up. Jessica had been spending so much time trying to get her life back on the right track. In the past few weeks, she hadn't even made time to hold a conversation with Brandon. It just so happened that at that moment, Brandon was coming her way.

"Here you go."

"What's this?"

"It's your notebook that you left in my locker a while back. I was doing my locker clean out."

"Oh, thank you. I can't believe this school year is ending already."

"Been a crazy year."

"Exactly."

"So how have you been? I haven't seen much of you around school."

"I've just been focusing on finishing my classes and passing these exams. Thanks for the notebook, Brandon. I gotta go."

"Sure, sure. Are you planning on coming to school tomorrow for the last day?"

"I'll be here."

"Ok, cool. Take care of yourself, Jessica."

"Thanks, you too."

Brandon was completely heartbroken! He wasn't sure anything could be done about it. He and Jessica were now in a completely different space. When Robin and Martin put Jessica on punishment, it disconnected her from a lot. Truthfully, she enjoyed this time away from her daily distractions, but it caused a major separation between her and some of her friendships. Jessica barely saw or spoke to Brandon and Kristen since the entire situation with Mr. McCall escalated. These were the two people who were there for Jessica to listen and support her. She needed that now more than ever. She needed her friends, but she also needed to be their friend and be there for them.

Jessica had been on punishment for the past seven weeks and she was hoping that her parents would allow her a few hours of free time so that she could clear the air with some people. Robin made herself very clear on multiple occasions when she said that Jessica would be on punishment up until the case was resolved in court. More than likely, neither she nor Martin would be giving in anytime soon. It was now almost summer vacation and Jessica needed to prove to her parents that she was ready for a job.

She wanted to work and start handling some responsibilities on her own. At her age, most people might wonder why she would want a job, but she felt that she needed to carry some of her own weight. Robin and Martin do very well for themselves, but Jessica really wanted to start becoming more independent. Tonight was the first night that Jessica was having dinner with both of her parents since they found out about Derrick McCall. Jessica thought it would be the best time to discuss the idea of her getting a job. Martin said that he would pick Robin and his daughter up for dinner so that they could all ride together. He was trying his best to keep their family unit strong.

"Your father is late, as always."

Robin was a very punctual person. She did not like to be late for anything! Most of the time, Martin and Jessica felt like she was a little too prompt, but they had learned to get used to it over the years.

"Who's ready for dinner?"

Martin quickly opened the front door. Jessica was hoping that she was not going to be the topic of discussion for the night, and she was hoping that her parents could keep the peace.

"DeLaney, you will be late to your own funeral."

"Well, they won't be able to start without me, so I think I'm good."

Robin wanted to laugh, but she held it in. Martin had this childish grin on his face that he always did since he and Robin had known one another. Jessica was just happy to be getting out of the house. They arrived at the restaurant within 45 minutes or so. To much surprise, the car ride went very well. Neither Martin nor Robin wanted to talk about the court case or anything along those lines, and they both knew that Jessica didn't want to either. It had been nearly two months and this was sort of the first time that Jessica had been anywhere. As far as she was concerned, she could stay out all night.

"My mom called earlier."

"How's she doing?"

"She's good, she's good. She was actually planning a summer vacation, and she wanted everyone to go. All three of us."

"Sylvia DeLaney will never understand the word divorce."

"Maybe if you dropped the last name, then she would get the picture." Martin laughed.

"Shut up."

Robin looked at Martin who had that same childish grin on his face. Honestly, she loved seeing Martin laugh and smile, but she would never admit that to her ex-husband. After being divorced for nearly four years, Robin was still hanging onto the DeLaney last name. She said it was for professional purposes, but Martin felt otherwise. Jessica was hoping that her parents would pass up the vacation because she wanted to get a job and start saving for an off-campus apartment when she went off to college in a little over a year. Robin and Martin were not aware of Jessica's plan, but she knew that if she presented them with money, then they may have a better understanding of what she was trying to accomplish.

"Jessica, you good? You sure are quiet."

"I'm fine."

"So what are your thoughts on this vacation? I think we all could use a little getaway, don't you?"

"I do, but I was hoping to stay in Houston and work this summer."

"Get a job?"

"Yeah. I wanted to start looking for one this week if I could."

"A job doesn't sound half bad."

"So I can get one?"

"It has to be one we approve of."

"I agree with your mother on that one. I got an idea! You can work at our offices."

"Work where you and mom work?"

"Yeah. You can work two days with me, two days with your mother, and you can have either a paid Friday or Monday off. Your choice."

"Just think, you won't even have to go through the crazy interview process," Robin added.

Jessica's plan was now ruined! Once again, her parents were doing anything they could to keep tabs on her at all times. She was willing to take less pay, work crazy hours, and work weekends just to be around other people that weren't Robin and Martin. Her idea of a job was maybe at a store at the mall or a local fast food restaurant. The only good part about working for her parents was that she would be able to go to the mall and shop for business attire.

"I was thinking of working at more of a public place, but if I am guaranteed employment with you guys, then I guess I can't pass that up."

"You can start after court."

From the moment that the morning announcements began, pictures were being taken and yearbooks being signed. Jessica was completely happy that she was ending such a difficult school year. She had gone from having it all figured out to questioning a lot of the situations that she was currently in, but Jessica was determined to make the best out of the situation. Her first order of business was to have a conversation with someone and end the tension between them for once and for all.

"Knock, knock."

"Come in. Hi, Jessica."

"Hi."

"Did you need something?"

"I wanted to speak to you if you had a minute or two."

"Have a seat."

"I just wanted to say that I felt like I should apologize for what went on between your husband and me."

"No need to go into details. Apology accepted."

"Ok. Now, don't you have one for me?"

"Excuse me?"

"For trying to use my father this past year, knowing you had your agenda all along."

"Little girl, who do you think you are?"

"I'm someone who can see right through you."

"You're someone who needs to remain in a child's place. Someone should have taught you that a long time ago. Then maybe you wouldn't be in the situation that you're in now."

"Are you questioning the way that my parents raised me?"

"I'm questioning your actions. Now, get out of this classroom."

"You will never accept the fact that your husband, the man that you love so deeply, did everything in his power to sleep with me."

"Is that so? I find it highly unlikely that a grown man would go after someone in your league."

"Well, maybe you don't know the person that you're married to all that well."

"Do not bring my personal affairs up again."

"I don't get it. You've lied to my father for an entire year! You even stopped wearing your engagement ring."

"What?"

"The ring that he was so proud of. The ring he couldn't wait to give to you."

"For the record, your father has never proposed to me. So maybe you were misinformed."

Jessica was confused because it had been months since her father had spoken to their family about wanting to make Lisa his wife. It was not anything that she was happy about, but she was going to support her father and his decision. She had no idea that he never went through with the proposal.

"Have a good summer, Lisa."

"Goodbye, Jessica."

Jessica should have minded her own business. She was embarrassed, but she was ready to move on from every painful memory from this school year. Grant it, she had some good memories, but it was now time to move on. She met a guy that she thought she would be with for the rest of her life. Brandon would always hold a special place in her heart. The two of them really meant a lot to one another, and this was probably the last summer that they would have to hang out and just be carefree. However, things were not going that well between them and because of that, Jessica wasn't too sure if the time was right for them to be spending more time with each other. She had a lot to do this summer.

The trial was scheduled to begin in about a week or so, her grandmother organized a family vacation, and she was planning to start her job soon. Today was her first day of freedom. Robin and Martin agreed to let Jessica go to the mall to shop for work clothes, but she had to be back home by nine that evening and not a minute later.

In Jessica's eyes, it felt weird because she had not been out publically in a very long time. She did not want to go shopping alone, but she hadn't patched things up with Kristen yet so she decided to hang out with someone that she thought would be worth getting to know better, and that was Olivia. Olivia had become a family friend over time and she really helped keep the peace during the entire situation. Jessica knew that she wouldn't constantly bring up court while they were shopping, and that was a relief. These two young ladies were both focused on rebuilding their lives.

Olivia was currently engaged to Mrs. Thompson's nephew. After their wedding, they were planning on starting their married life in Houston as opposed to remaining in San Antonio. She had been spending a lot of time in the area, and the DeLaney family welcomed her with open arms. After dealing with Derrick McCall, it took Olivia a very long time to step into a relationship. For a while, it felt strange for her to have someone love her the right way. Olivia was a proud fiancé and what made her even more proud was that she took her life back.

"So, is the wedding planning almost done?"

"Just about. Hopefully, all I have to do now is show up."

"If only it were that easy." Jessica laughed.

Jessica was a bit more mature than most people her age. She always tried her best to look at things in the most positive light. Ever since the situation, Jessica felt as if her time was up at Lenwood High School. She was considering transferring to a nearby High School, but she wasn't too sure that her parents would agree with her plan. It wasn't that she was trying to run away from her past, but she wanted to have a fresh start. Grant it, that's what college would be for.

"Olivia, I wrote Mr. McCall a letter."

"You didn't."

"I did."

"Why?"

"I felt like I had to release some of the anger that was still inside of me."

"Please don't tell me that you gave it to him."

"He has the letter."

Olivia's jaw dropped! Although Jessica was mature for her age, she still was a little naive in certain situations.

"Jessica, don't you know that he could use that as evidence that you're still trying to communicate with him?"

"I felt like I had to release that anger."

"I get that, believe me, I do. I just feel that maybe you shouldn't have given him the letter."

Jessica quickly realized that she had made a mistake that could possibly come back and smack her in the face. She wanted to crawl into a hole and hide, but once again, it was now her responsibility to deal with the mistakes she made.

"Do you think that he'll bring it to court?"

"Figuring Derrick McCall out is nearly impossible. Now that he has Lisa giving her input, there's no telling what might happen."

Jessica instantly went into kid mode. She was worried sick that Derrick would say she was the one still contacting him. Her parents would be livid if they knew that she was still trying to contact her former teacher.

"I messed up."

"Yes, but it's ok."

Olivia could see the vulnerable side of Jessica. Not that there was anything wrong that she was still vulnerable, but she wanted Jessica to move past all of the unnecessary drama in her life. As for Jessica, she wanted to burst into tears, but she had business to take care of. From here on out, nothing would be easy. For now, she was going to enjoy this shopping day and then head over to see her Attorney. She hadn't met with the team in a while, but she was sure that her mother was staying on top of everything and making sure it was all taken care of. Later at the meeting, Jessica thought that she would show up early to get some personal time with her lawyer before her parents showed up, but they beat her to the punch.

"Hey, Jess."

"Hi everybody."

"Jessica, how have you been?"

"I've been ok, thanks."

Jessica's lawyer was one of the best in her practice. She was committed to any case that she took on and she was very proactive. The DeLaney family truly trusted this team, and they believed that Derrick McCall would get what he really deserved.

"So, the trial is set to begin soon. The only thing that I would like to say is that I have seen cases like these go either way. I have seen people serve long-term sentencing, but I have also seen some become eligible for parole within such a short amount of time."

"His ass better get life!" Martin interrupted.

"From a parents' perspective, I can completely understand, but I don't think a life sentence will be happening. Uh, Martin is Lisa saying anything? Have you spoken to her about it?"

"I haven't been in contact with her."

Martin and Lisa's relationship was completely finished. Martin was focusing on Jessica and shaping her for the future. He and Robin both wanted to control what went on in their daughter's life, but they knew that pretty soon that would no longer be the case.

"Well," their attorney continued, "Martin if you were to speak to Lisa, do not discuss anything! Don't mention anything to anyone for that matter. It would just be best if no one discussed this trial."

Jessica wanted to cringe! The only thing playing in her head was the conversation that she had with Lisa on the last day of school. Truthfully, the conversation could have very well been avoided, but that was Jessica's fault for pushing the limits. She had been thinking a lot about what Olivia had said earlier, and she was upset that she even wrote the letter to begin with. Jessica wanted to convince herself that she was done with Derrick McCall, but she knew that there was still something about him that gave her butterflies. The entire situation was heartbreaking, but it was time for everyone to deal with the task at hand.

Chutney and McCall hadn't seen one another since Derrick was taken into custody for questioning. Chutney went with Lisa to post bail, but he did not stick around to see his friend once he was released. Anyone who knew these two would consider this behavior to be unusual. Anthony Chutney and Derrick McCall grew up together in Atlanta, Georgia. They were on the same sports teams, they went to the same High School, and they both are products of Morehouse. Chutney relocated to Houston a few years ago. At the time, he had been teaching for nine years. Derrick landed a job in San Antonio and left last year when he suspected his past involvement with Olivia was coming back to haunt him. That is when Chutney hired him at Lenwood, not knowing his reason for leaving his previous school. Derrick hadn't been doing much with his spare time since he was suspended from work. Now that school was over, he was starting one of the most dreadful summers he would ever have. He was watching the NBA Semi-Finals when he heard a knock. To his surprise, it was his best friend.

"What's up?"

"Nothing much, man."

"You got a few minutes?"

Derrick backed up so that Chutney could walk in.

"Want a beer or something?"

"I'll have a cold one with you."

You could see on Derrick's face that he wasn't the happiest person, and he still had some questions for his best friend, but he was going to wait and see what Chutney's visit was all about.

"I know you probably thought I was dodging you or something."

"Nah. I know you have to play your role."

"Play my role?"

"You're the Principal, and like you said, you have a job to do. I can't argue with you there, and our brotherhood can't compete with that."

Chutney had made up his mind that he wasn't going to personally involve himself in this situation, but he was going to handle the responsibilities that he has as a serving Principal. His first act was to suspend McCall until all of these allegations were settled.

"Lisa told you that she came to talk to me?"

"Something like that. I'm not trying to involve my wife in any of this anymore. That's why I asked her to go visit her parents until all of this was done."

"You sure you don't want your wife by your side?"

"I'm not about to let anyone else try to get her to change her perception of me based on a mistake."

"You think she's going to leave you again?"

"Lisa stood by me then and she's standing by me now. I just thought that I would have a few more people in my corner."

"You talking about me?"

Derrick did not respond right away.

"Twenty-five years! You've been my brother, my best friend, my best man at my wedding, and my boss! All of a sudden you go ghost over some alleged accusations."

"D. Man, I knew there was still some investigating going on. I didn't want to cause any confusion."

"If this had happened to me at any other school and you heard about it, you would be right by me every step of the way."

"You trying to say that I chose my job over my best friend? Come on, McCall, that's some female bullshit! At Lenwood, I'm the Principal and that's what it is. As Principal, my job is to protect not only my staff but also the entire student body."

"So who did you choose to protect?"

"I came to you months ago and asked you to be upfront with me."

"It shouldn't have to be that way! My best friend shouldn't second guess my character!"

Chutney and McCall were brothers as far as they were concerned, and Chutney could always tell when Derrick was withholding information. It hurt him that he wasn't getting the truth from the person that he would trust with his life. He couldn't look at Derrick the same way that he once did, and he was trying really hard not to let this come between their friendship. Chutney wanted the trial to be done and for everyone to move on with their lives. In life, there are mistakes and in life there are consequences.

"Remember when you graduated High School? Your Pops said, *"Son – as long as you're solid with your brother, you're set for life."* Just know that I got you near or far, McCall."

Chutney left and neither one of them knew if they would ever be on the same page again. McCall knew that he and Anthony would always be brothers, but this was a lot to swallow. At the end of the day, his friend had a job to do, a family to feed, and he didn't want to compromise any of that. Derrick sat there and reality started to sink in. He had made a really big mistake and was now on the front page of all of the local newspapers with the caption **"STATUTORY RAPIST"** below. Derrick began to cry. He hadn't cried throughout this entire situation, but there was more and more going on. Court was now a couple of days away and all he could focus on was life after he left that courtroom. It would never be the same from then on. An hour later, Derrick received another knock on the door. The last thing he was ready for was another visit, but he just assumed that it was Lisa returning home early.

"Hello."

"What's going on?"

"I know that this shouldn't be happening, but I really wanted to talk to you if I could."

Jessica was swimming in the deep end yet again. She showed up to Derrick's home and this should have been the last place that she came to once she was released from her punishment.

"This is crazy! What are you trying to do? Send me away for life?"

"I just need a few minutes of your time, please."

The biggest mistake Derrick made was letting Jessica inside of his home and he knew that. He was taking a big risk, but at this point, he felt as if he should hear what she had to say.

"Thank you."

"So what's going on?"

"I know that you got the letter that I sent with everything."

"Yeah."

"Although I'm only 17, I can't place the blame on you only. Over the course of this year, I have certainly played my part in this situation. Today all I wanted to do was end my school year right. I know that I said everything in that letter, but out of respect for you, I wanted to personally let you know that I am moving past all of this."

"I get the message, Jessica."

"Thanks."

Derrick walked towards the door so that he could see Jessica out, but she didn't budge.

"Wait."

"What now?"

"There's more."

Derrick didn't want to hear anything else that Jessica had to say. He certainly did not want anyone to see her leave his house. Martin and Robin were trying to trust their daughter again the way they once did, and they were tempted to place a tracking device in her car. Luckily for her, they hadn't done so.

"Jessica, whatever you have to say, can you make it quick?"

"I'm sorry. Didn't mean to frustrate you."

"I'm not frustrated, but I have quite a few pending charges filed by your family and the state. We do not need to be communicating."

"You have sex with me over and over, but now all of a sudden I'm the only one at fault?"

"Did I ever force you to sleep with me?"

"I was manipulated!"

"Excellent Attorney, she coached you well. So I guess you were manipulated when you decided to come by here tonight when you know you shouldn't have?"

"Maybe it was my choice. Maybe I wanted it one last time. Maybe I crave you and the sexual attention that only you can give to me."

Jessica walked towards Derrick. He looked confused and he felt uncomfortable. Derrick knew that he needed to open his front door and escort Jessica out, but he also knew that it would draw more attention to his home. That was exactly what he did not need.

"Jessica."

"Do you know what it took to get here? Do you know that I'm risking everything just by being in your house right now?"

She was ignoring everything that Derrick was trying to say. She was fighting against rejection. All she wanted was to have her way with this man "one last time".

"Jessica, you have to go out the back way."

"So soon? I have two hours until I have to be home."

"You are a child!"

"Was I a child when we were in San Antonio? Was I a child when I was on top of you when we were up in your room? Look, Lisa's not here and we all know that you need this before you go in."

McCall was so tempted to satisfy his needs as a man, but he knew that this was not right. Jessica groped Mr. McCall slowly and kissed his neck. Who would believe that this young lady would put herself into the same situation that her parents have been trying to save her from? In less than 72 hours, the dirty laundry would be aired. Derrick still had not mentally prepared himself for incarceration. Truthfully, he had mentally checked out from the moment that he was escorted away from Lenwood High School. Everything was now a blur, but somehow Jessica ended up on McCall's kitchen counter. The cereal box slammed to the floor, pieces of mail were thrown, and McCall's bottoms were leading a trail into the living room. The passion, the attraction- it was ALL WRONG! Jessica was having the time of her life, and it didn't take much for a teenager to fall in love. She wanted McCall to have his way with her – one last time.

# CHAPTER 10

# THE ADVOCATE

"This is really hard not being there in Houston right now."

"Baby, it's all going to be fine."

"What if I don't get to see you and they take you away?"

"We're not going to worry about all of that. Our main focus is to make sure that our marriage survives. You know that we're built to last."

"I'm still convinced that I need to be in that courtroom. Is Chut going?"

"He'll be there. I just don't know if he'll be there in my defense. He stopped by the other night."

"What did he say?"

"Basically he told me that he had a job to do."

"So a 25-year friendship doesn't mean shit to him?"

"He didn't say that."

"That's what he was trying to say."

"Lisa, I'm going to get some sleep. I'll call you in the morning."

"I love you, Derrick."

"I love you and I mean it."

It was the night before the trial date and reality was starting to sink in for everyone involved. Derrick had to defend himself against the young lady that begged him to sleep with her just 48 hours ago. He couldn't sleep, but if he would have stayed on the phone with Lisa then he would have been crushed! His heart couldn't handle it. Derrick's mother was a praying woman and she called her son each morning for scripture and prayer. It broke her heart that her son didn't want his family present in court, but they all had agreed to respect his wishes. In 24 hours, one story would be told from multiple perspectives.

"Babe, shouldn't you be asleep?"

"I can't."

"Thinking about tomorrow?"

"Yeah. You think I want to see my best friend, my brother be taken away?"

"I wish I could feel your pain. Look, I love Derrick, he's family, the godfather to our children, but I just don't recognize this Derrick."

"Me neither."

Jae is Chutney's wife. She had been around Derrick for the last twelve years, and she knew the relationship that her husband had with his best friend. This situation opened up so many different questions and concerns. Jae wasn't sure if she wanted her daughters around their Uncle Derrick for the time being.

"I went to see him the other night."

"How'd it go?"

"He wasn't cool. He was really upset that I hadn't been by the house since this whole situation took place."

"Does he not understand your position?"

"I guess he doesn't." Chutney shrugged.

"Trying to determine your loyalty is something he shouldn't even be doing. We have children to raise and a household to maintain even when all of this is over."

It hurt Chutney more and more to think about tomorrow. He had to be both Principal Chutney and "Ant". He wasn't too sure if he could wear both hats. He loved his job, and he loved to protect his staff and student body. This was a situation that he couldn't wait to come to an end.

Jessica had gotten up early and was ready to go hours before they were expected to be in the courtroom. She was hoping to ride alone to the trial, but she knew that her parents wouldn't agree. All that she could think about was the other night when she visited Derrick Mc-Call. Although it never should have happened, Jessica did not regret it. She could not help that she connected well with a man on so many different levels. She knew that today her parents would find out more about the situation than they had hoped for. All that was on her mind was how she would be looked at once it was all over.

"Sweetheart, don't you think you should eat something?"

"I'm not hungry right now, Ma."

"Here's a bottle of water. Your dad just sent me a message saying that he's out front."

The drive to the courthouse was about 25 minutes, and Jessica knew it would feel longer than that. She sat quietly in the backseat next to her grandmother. No one said anything as the radio played. Martin was trying to remain calm. Today would be the first day that he would be face-to-face with Derrick McCall. He was unsure about how he would react, but he knew that he had to maintain his composure.

"You don't understand how sick I feel right now! They can't take you away from me."

"Lisa, calm down. You know that I love you and that's what matters. All I can hope is that you can stand by me through this."

"I'll stand by you regardless, but I don't think you should be facing a situation like this all alone."

"I got me and my attorneys got me."

"Does Chut?"

"Chut has a job to do."

It bothered Lisa that the people who should have stayed by Derrick's side had now disappeared during the heat. Truthfully, she regretted everything that they went through in their marriage. It was as if this was all payback for Lisa trying to take half of Martin's business. These two were made for one another. Both Derrick and Lisa have had their share of difficult times, but now it was time to face the music.

"Don't be nervous, and don't say too much right away. Simple yes and no answers will do." Derrick's attorney was giving last minute advice.

Derrick just nodded. He sat on the opposite side of the courtroom with his head down. Jessica sat to the far right with her lawyer. Mrs.

Thompson and Principal Chutney were in attendance and to much surprise, Kristen and Brandon were there as well. Kristen genuinely wanted some closure for her best friend. Despite how thick the tension had been, she still wanted everything to work out for the best. If she knew that Jessica had still been communicating with Derrick, let alone having sex with him, she would reevaluate their friendship. Brandon was honestly there because he still had feelings for Jessica. He wanted all of the details about her involvement with Mr. McCall, but he wasn't sure if he was prepared for the truth. Brandon still gave Jessica butterflies inside, but she was not interested in a relationship. The minute this trial ended would be one of the happiest days of her life, but she knew that she would have to accept responsibility for her part.

"All rise!"

Everyone stood as Judge Kitt entered the courtroom. McCall and Jessica were standing with their attorneys and now things were about to get real.

"Mr. McCall, when did you first begin working at Lenwood High school?"

"August of last year."

"Prior to last August, did you know Miss DeLaney?"

"No ma'am."

"Thank you. Miss DeLaney, you stated that you have just completed your junior year in High School."

"Yes."

"In the prior years, have you seen Mr. McCall out or had any contact with him prior to last year?"

"No, Your Honor."

"Attorney, please bring forth your first witness."

Jessica's attorney asked Principal Chutney to approach the stand.

"Thank you. Your Honor, at this time I would like to call Anthony Chutney to the stand."

Once he was sworn in, Chutney sat down and immediately broke out into a sweat. He was numb! As an educator, he was prepared to protect his staff and students at all costs. He knew that what his best friend did was wrong, but he was just not used to seeing his best friend being compared to these rapists of the world. It didn't sit well. He couldn't grasp the reality.

"Mr. Chutney, how long have you known Mr. McCall?"

"25 years."

"So the two of you must be pretty close. Is it true that the two of you refer to one another as brothers?"

"Yes."

"So typically that means that you would tell one another just about everything. My question to you is: How could you not suspect unusual behavior between your best friend of 25 years and a student in the school where you serve as the Principal?"

"Their interactions did not seem unusual around me."

"Did your student ask you to attend yearbook meetings?"

"Some of them."

"And that didn't seem like a cry for help?"

"Not at the time."

"No further questions. Your witness."

McCall put his head down for a quick second. He should have known that Jessica's lawyer would come to fight! They were not going to rest until he was locked away in a jail cell forever. He felt bad that he put his best friend in such a compromising position. This was the man who made things happen when McCall wanted to relocate to a new school. Chutney never asked for a reason, but maybe he should have back then. At the time, he was just looking out for his friend, but it ended up being a very difficult situation. The court took a recess, and McCall went to talk more with his attorneys. On the way out, he saw Olivia had walked back into the courthouse. SHOTS FIRED! Derrick knew that Olivia's presence was of ill intent, but he could not draw any connection between Olivia and Jessica. He didn't see Olivia at the hotel when they were in San Antonio, but he knew exactly what team she was up to bat for.

"I'm not going out without putting up a fight!"

"We're going to go back in with every piece of information that we have."

"I have something else."

Derrick had something that would sort of help his name. However, nothing would save him from the fact that he slept with this student. When the case resumed, Olivia took the stand. She had never imagined that she would be telling her truth after nearly eight years. As promised, she kept her word and was there in support of Jessica, but she was unaware that Jessica did not keep her promise about staying away from Derrick McCall.

"Miss Sollers, what High School did you attend?"

"Langley High School."

"During your time at Langley, did you have the unfortunate pleasure of having Mr. McCall as your teacher?"

"My Sophomore and Junior year."

"Can you tell the court your opinion of him as a teacher?"

"He was very engaging and was always willing to help his students."

Olivia was being neutral, and no one could really figure out if she was going to spit out the truth about her involvement with Mr. McCall.

"Miss Sollers, did you ever spend one-on-one time with your former teacher, Mr. McCall?"

"I have."

"Did any of this happen outside of the classroom?"

"Yes."

Before responding, Olivia took a brief silence. She was beginning to realize that the end was near. Pretty soon, the verdict would be determined.

"Did you two have sex with one another?"

Olivia looked Derrick in the eyes, "We did. We did for about six months."

"No further questions."

The room was silent and Martin was DISGUSTED! He wanted to slam Derrick against the wall and choke him to death. Truth be told, he was speaking out of anger, but there was no sympathetic bone in his body at that moment. Derrick's lawyer called Jessica to the stand; she was the last person to testify.

"Miss DeLaney, aside from the yearbook meetings, you have admitted to spending time with my client."

"Yes."

"After watching the security cameras from the hotel, you stated that Mr. McCall had forced you to spend time with him, but the way you were dressed in that video heading down the hallway said something else. I feel the Jury would agree once the video is viewed."

Jessica began to get nervous! They started to zoom in on the security tape and right there, clear as day, you could see Jessica dressed in the nightgown that she had taken from her mother's closet. Robin remembered a certain gown that was missing from her closet months ago. Tears began to form in her eyes. Her daughter was showing a completely different side of her and Jessica could not say a word. She was so embarrassed! Although the two were no longer together, she felt as if she had betrayed Brandon. He knew about what went on in San Antonio, but he had no idea about what McCall's lawyer was prepared to do next.

"Miss DeLaney, the moment this case went under investigation, you were told to stay away from my client. Am I correct?"

"Yes."

"That normally means no type of contact would be accepted."

"Yes."

"So if all of those orders were in place, why were you still in contact with Mr. McCall?"

"I wasn't."

"Is that so? Ms. DeLaney, please remember you are under oath. My client felt like you would say that. That is why I would like to present the court with this! Your Honor, I present to you a letter written by Miss DeLaney that was mailed to my client. Here are some photos of Miss DeLaney's vehicle parked close to my client's home. If that does not suffice, I have a detailed conversation that was recorded by my client. It is him and Miss DeLaney talking. This recording dates back to less than 72 hours ago when Miss DeLaney showed up at my client's home without him being aware that she was coming."

"OBJECTION! Your Honor, there is no proof that the vehicle pictured belongs to my client."

"This document is proof that the vehicle pictured is registered to Robin DeLaney, Miss DeLaney's mother."

"Do something!" Martin shouted.

"Order, order in the court! Let us resume tomorrow morning at 9 AM. You all are dismissed."

The Judge exited the courtroom and Jessica was in tears. This was like a movie scene, but a horrible one. Both Brandon and Kristen had no idea that things would go this far when they first decided to go to Mrs. Thompson and fill her in about what Jessica had been doing. Robin and Martin were both heartbroken. Their family had seen the most difficult times and this was another chapter in the horror story. Jessica walked out of the courthouse with her head down and sunglasses on. She walked past McCall and his lawyers. Suddenly, her body got really warm. Slowly, she entered her father's SUV and they drove away. Martin and Robin were too hurt and betrayed to even say a word to their daughter. The entire ride home was silent. Robin tried to gather her thoughts. She knew that she had to have a conversation with her daughter, but she did not want to be upset when she did it.

"Robin, I'm telling you right now, I don't know how much more I can take."

"So, what now? Are you going to run because things are getting tough?"

"Don't make this about us."

"This is about us, Martin! We are responsible for everything that goes on with that girl upstairs."

"Robin, don't you think I know that? I love her more than myself. I would give my life so that my son could be here too, but I can't! I can't have him and my daughter here forever. That's how my life worked out, but you better believe that I'm going to work overtime to make sure that my daughter is protected."

"I'm not too sure if I even want her back at Lenwood to be honest.

I just don't think we as parents were fully supported by their Administration."

"What did you expect? This man is damn near Principal Chutney's brother. There's no telling where his loyalty lies."

"I would hope that he would still play his role. As Principal, he should have been more vocal. I had to make all of the phone calls that should have been made to me."

"Just the way it is."

Robin and Martin both agreed that they wouldn't discuss anything with Jessica that night. The two of them needed time to calm down and really think about what was going on so that they could respond the correct way. Jessica couldn't sleep that night. She tossed and turned for hours and finally decided to stay up for the remainder of the night. When Jeremiah, Jessica's brother passed away, she had no one to talk to about how it all made her feel. Her parents were dealing with the loss individually and collaboratively, but Jessica felt as if her emotions did not matter. Her solution to the problem was to write letters to her deceased brother. For Jessica, it was therapeutic and it would help her with the healing process.

*Dear Jeremiah,*

*I know that if you were here, you would be too young to understand what I was going through, but I know that you would help make me stronger just by me being in your presence. I still cry for you at night, and I just wish I could hold you again. Your big sister really messed up, but I am doing my best to try and fix it. I am going to do my best to look after mom and dad. Your death has ruined all of us, but we are trying our best to go on with our lives. I feel like we have known you for a lifetime, although it was a short while. Just know that you will always be in our hearts.*

*Love,*

*Jessica*

Today was the day that Derrick would be sentenced. He hated that he had to play dirty, but he felt that everyone involved needed to accept responsibility for the role that they have played throughout this situation. He knew that he would be entering a jail cell today most likely, and he left everything for Lisa to handle.

"All rise-"

The moment that the Bailiff began to speak, the room became silent. Everyone stood up until the Judge allowed them to be seated.

"All witnesses have verbally stated their perspectives as well as given written statements. I have had the opportunity to view videos, listen to recordings, and the verdict is in. Mr. McCall, please stand."

Derrick stood up.

"While the evidence provided by you and your defense team weighed heavily on my decision, what went on was sickening! It is statutory rape! I am sentencing you to ten years with all but five years suspended. It is imperative that you serve a minimum of two and a half years in Federal Prison before you can become eligible for a parole hearing. Any questions?"

"No, Your Honor."

"At this time, I am going to turn you over into the custody of the Houston Sherriff Department."

They handcuffed Derrick and everyone watched as he was escorted out of the courtroom. Martin and Robin were not satisfied with the Judge's decision. The reality was that McCall could potentially be released from prison before Jessica would even finish college. It was all over, but it all still seemed unsettled. The Judge ordered that Jessica should not complete her twelfth-grade year at Lenwood High School. Truthfully, Jessica was happy because she could now move on and have a fresh start. When they got back to the house, Robin and Martin decided that they needed to have a long, overdue conversation with their daughter about everything that transpired over the past year.

"Jess, I just want to say that this was one of the most devastating experiences as a parent for me, and of course hearing more things than we were aware of didn't help how we felt from the beginning."

"I know."

"Why would you betray us again? Do you know what you did?"

You could hear the anger in Martin's voice. He couldn't stop seeing the videos of Derrick and Jessica in his head. It nearly brought tears to his eyes.

"I can't do anything but constantly apologize. I'm sorry, but I promise that going forward I will never make this mistake again."

"Well, your father and I will try our best to trust your word."

Jessica decided to go up to her room. It had been an emotional week and she was exhausted! This had been a dreadful year, but she was ready to move on with her life. Now that she would no longer be attending Lenwood, she still felt obligated to clear the air with Kristen and Brandon and to see where those friendships would go from here on out.

Lisa was now back in town from her visit with her parents, and it was time to continue life while her husband was serving his jail time. The facility was only an hour away so Lisa would more than likely make every visit. She wasn't there for the trial, so she asked Chutney to meet up with her and fill her in on what all went on in the courtroom. Anthony was still feeling uneasy about the situation, especially on Jessica's behalf. Still, he felt as if Derrick deserved a loyal friend if nothing else. He also wanted to reach out to the DeLaney family when the timing was right.

"Chut, I know the sentence could have been a lot worse, but I am still worried."

"Well, I feel like the Judge felt that everyone involved should be held accountable for their actions."

"That's understood. You of all people know that I love Derrick, but this definitely puts a strain on our relationship."

"Wasn't their infidelity on both sides?"

"Correct, but mine wasn't illegal."

"Right now he needs our support so that he can complete those counseling programs."

"It's a nightmare! It's like I don't even know my husband right now."

"To be a young educator is already a risk. The fact that you're closer to the students' ages makes others assume that you're interested. It's our job to beat those odds."

"Well, I guess my husband didn't beat those odds."

"You're sounding like you're giving up."

"Giving up? Giving up on what? Giving up on who? My marriage? My husband?"

"Maybe I misjudged your tone."

"You did. Come on, Chut. I know that my marriage has been any-thing but easy, but you of all people know that I love my husband and I am committed, despite all of our mistakes in the past."

"You're right. I'm going to check with Angela Thompson and see if she's been in contact with the DeLaney family."

"Why?"

"I just want to make sure that they understand that the staff at Len-wood did everything we could to support their family."

"And you trust Angela to handle all of that?"

"I'm going to handle it, but she's going to assist."

"The same ex-fiancé that turned into your colleague."

"We've both moved on."

"I get it, but it's crazy how no one knew about your relationship with her. Derrick didn't even know."

"We were young and I still wanted to play that bachelor role. It was a mistake that I wish would have never happened, but we have moved on."

"You think that she was so determined to see Derrick go down so that she could get back at you? Or maybe she wanted to hurt him be-cause she believed that he's the reason why you cheated on her when the two of you were engaged."

"Good point," Anthony laughed.

"Derrick and I need your motivation, Chut. We need it now and we'll need it long after he's released. I know that Derrick has made a big mistake, but you are his brother and we have always valued your love and support."

This entire situation had humbled Lisa in such a short period of time. She also played a malicious role in this without even knowing it, but she was ready to move forward. Now she was more focused on being a supportive wife and holding down this relationship while her husband was away.

Jessica made it a priority to meet up with Kristen over the summer so that they could possibly repair their fractured friendship. For almost four years, Jessica and Kristen had been the best of friends, but this past year was definitely a test. Jessica wanted to say her apologies, and she was hoping that this would not be the last conversation between these two.

"Hey, Jess."

"Hey! Thanks for meeting me here."

"Sure."

Kristen had been through a lot in her life, and that had all taught her not to take everything in life so personal. Jessica was not always invested in their friendship as much as Kristen, but it was never held against her.

"I just wanted to say thank you for being there in court for me. Uh, the support from you and Brandon has been everything I needed. I know that I really was mad at the two of you for going to Mrs. Thompson, but only real friends would do that for me. I just wanted to apologize for not being the friend that I should have been to you."

Jessica was becoming more and more selfless, and she was beginning to accept her faults. She was grateful that she would be attending a new High School because it was now time to move on.

"Jess, you will always be my sister. We have dealt with so much that we overlook the simple fact that we are still teenagers with so much growing to do. If nothing else, we know that we will always hold each other down whether we are near or far."

This was most likely their last conversation for a while. Jessica appreciated Kristen's honesty and she knew that their friendship would always last. It was now time to become the best versions of themselves.

Finally, it was time that Jessica had a long-awaited conversation with Brandon. When she left her lunch with Kristen, Jessica immediately went to meet with him. Their relationship was difficult to understand because it never officially ended. Brandon could really see himself with Jessica for the rest of his life, but he wasn't sure if he could look past everything that went on with Mr. McCall. The two of them met up at the park nearby Lenwood and there was an awkward silence from the start.

"Hey."

"Hey, give me a hug. Good to see you."

"Good to see you too. Thanks for meeting me here."

"Of course."

Brandon was happy to hear from Jessica, but he did not want to show all of his excitement right way. Jessica was mesmerized by the scent of his cologne and it distracted her for a moment. She had a lot that she needed to say, but she wanted to enjoy the infatuation first.

"Umm, I was telling Kristen how I really appreciated the two of you being there for all of my mess in court. I know that I was upset with you guys in the beginning, but the two of you did exactly what needed to be done."

"I never thought we would be in separate schools for our last year of High School."

"Neither did I. You know, I have had so many great things happen at Lenwood, but I am so ready to move on."

"Move on, move on?"

"Huh?"

"When you say move on, do you mean into a new relationship?"

"Oh, no. That's not even on my mind right now. I have spent all summer saving up for a college apartment. I want to enjoy my senior year and just make memories."

"I hope that I can be included in some of those memories."

"Me too."

"Take care of yourself, Jessica. I love you."

They hugged and Brandon left. Jessica was at peace now and she could not wait to see him again. For now, she just wanted to focus on getting her life back on track. She learned a lot about so many people in her life, and she was learning to appreciate all of the simple things.

Derrick was now receiving counseling services in prison. So far, he and Lisa were able to keep their marriage strong. She got to visit three times a month for two hours. In their eyes, it was never enough, but they were going to continue to stick by one another.

Chutney was working on bettering his staff at Lenwood High School for the remainder of the summer. He had to hire a new English teacher and he had such high expectations for the school moving forward. He chose to visit Derrick often because in his eyes, they were still brothers and he was going to stick by him through the difficult times. Robin and Martin were still going to their therapy sessions. They were doing better in dealing with their son's death and their divorce. It had been a very difficult few years, but they were ready to focus on all of what Jessica had ahead of her. Everyone was headed in separate directions and moving on from such a hurtful situation. It was time to prepare for what was to come. Jessica had a voice in this world and it was now her time to use it.

- *Tyeashia M. Hurley*

Interested in Writing and/or Publishing a book?
Contact: www.a2zbookspublishing.net

9 781943 284436